THE DOUGHBOYS OVER THERE

RUSSIA

AUSTRIA-HUNGARY

Vienna ★

SOLDIERS
ON THE
BATTLEFRONT

THE DOUGHBOYS OVER THERE

SOLDIERING IN WORLD WAR I

RUSSIA

AUSTRIA-HUNGARY

Susan Provost Beller

Vienna ✪

Twenty-First Century Books • Minneapolis

To the first of my "in-law kids," Joanne Gaudette

Title page image: American Doughboys wait next to a bunker.

Twenty-First Century Books
A division of Lerner Publishing Group, Inc.
241 First Avenue North
Minneapolis, MN 55401 U.S.A.

Website address: www.lernerbooks.com

Library of Congress Cataloging-in-Publication Data

Beller, Susan Provost, 1949–
    The doughboys over there : soldiering in World War I / by Susan Provost Beller.
        p.   cm. — (Soldiers on the battlefront)
    Includes bibliographical references and index.
    ISBN-13: 978-0–8225–6295–5 (lib. bdg. : alk. paper)
    ISBN-10: 0–8225–6295–2 (lib. bdg. : alk. paper)
        1. World War, 1914–1918—United States—Juvenile literature. 2. Soldiers—United States—
Social conditions—20th century—Juvenile literature. 3. World War, 1914–1918—France—
Juvenile literature. I. Title.
    D570.B44 2008
    940.4'0973—dc22   2006026249

Manufactured in the United States of America
1 2 3 4 5 6 — JR — 13 12 11 10 09 08

Contents

"Time Will Not Dim the Glory of Their Deeds."

—Monument to the Doughboys in France

"Time Will Not Dim the Glory of Their Deeds." These are the words on the

PROLOGUE

monument to the American Doughboy just two miles outside of Château-Thierry, France. It has been a lonely place since the Doughboys have passed on. Their role in World War I (1914–1918) has been somewhat forgotten.

The deeds of the Doughboys have been overshadowed by the soldiers of World War II (1939–1945). Yet, soldiers of both wars fought and died on the same soil in France. The actions of the supporters and enemies of the Doughboys are also frequently overlooked. World War I is often called the forgotten war.

WORLD WAR 1 BEGINS

In the early 1900s, most of the countries in Europe were involved in a web of alliances and petty conflicts. On June 28, 1914, Archduke Franz Ferdinand of Austria was assassinated in Sarajevo, Serbia. Germany and Austria-Hungary were furious about Ferdinand's death because he was the heir to the throne of Austria-Hungary.

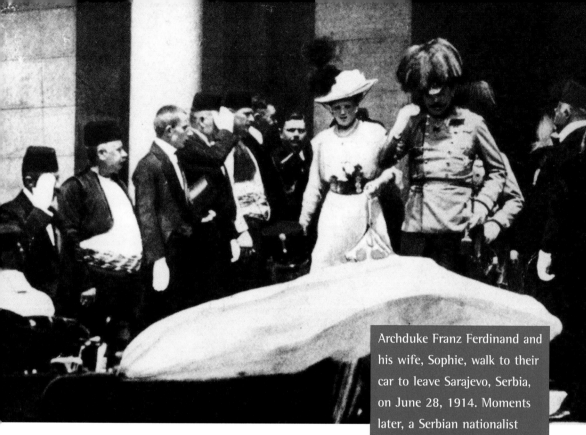

Austria-Hungary responded to the assassination with demands on the Serbian government. The Serbian government accepted most of the demands. However, the Serbian government would not allow Austria to provide agents to conduct the investigation of the assassination. They said this violated their national independence. Austria immediately declared war, and armies began to gather. The chances for a peaceful resolution were lost.

Warfare broke out in August 1914. The conflict involved nearly all of Europe. The main countries involved were Great Britain, France, Russia, and later the United States. This group was known as the Allies. They fought the Central powers, which included Germany, Austria-Hungary, and the Ottoman Empire.

Some historians blame Germany and Austria-Hungary for the war. Their harsh response to the assassination led to their declaration of war. Other historians believe that war was inevitable among the European countries. They say the spark that started it could have come from any action at the time.

At first the war was viewed with great excitement in Europe. It was expected to be a short conflict, lasting only a few months at most. The United States initially refused to take sides.

The expectations for a short war, however, were proved wrong. The fighting dragged on into 1917. The war entered a stalemate. Armies faced one another in a well-developed series of trenches (defensive pits). This series of trenches was called the western front.

In 1917 the United States entered the war. The American Doughboy was called upon to move the war out of the trenches and to a conclusion.

REPAYING A DEBT

"Lafayette, we are here," said U.S. colonel C. E. Stanton. Stanton was part of commanding general John J. Pershing's staff. He was standing at the tomb of the Marquis de Lafayette, an eighteenth-century French general and statesman. In 1777 Lafayette had helped George Washington during the American Revolution (1775–1783). He served as a general in Washington's struggling army, and he served without pay. Washington's army won the war.

George Washington gave his farewell address at the end of his second term as U.S. president. He cautioned the people of the young nation to avoid becoming involved in Europe's politics and wars. However, he said that there was one exception—an "extraordinary emergency."

About 140 years had passed since Lafayette had offered his services to America. In the years since the Revolution, the United States had grown into a strong country. It had mostly stayed out of conflicts in Europe. But the United States hadn't forgotten how Lafayette and his country supported them. It considered France a strong ally.

In 1917 the situation in Europe became an emergency. Millions of troops had already died, and there was no end in sight. The American Doughboys began to arrive in France by the hundreds of thousands. They wanted to repay their debt to Lafayette and "make the world safe for democracy." The Allies hoped the Doughboys would finally turn the tide.

Almost one hundred years have passed since the first American Doughboys set foot on French soil. In that time, the United States changed from a neutral nation that avoided taking on an interna-tional role. It has become the most powerful nation in the world. But it all began with the Doughboys, fighting and dying "over there" in France.

> " Sheer exhaustion was slowly gaining the upper hand with us. Continual shelling, the constant necessity of removing debris, and deepening our miserable defences."
>
> —British officer I. L. Read, 1917

CHAPTER ONE

CHAPTER ONE
WHY THE DOUGHBOYS WENT TO FRANCE

To understand why the Allies on the western front needed the United States, visitors only need to go to the Douaumont Ossuary in Douaumont, France. This chapel of bones is located where the worst fighting of World War I took place. It is an impressive and moving place to begin any story of the war.

Visitors enter a chapel that is lined with marble slabs. The slabs name the military units of the 130,000 unknown French soldiers who are buried there. Even the loudest school groups hush as they enter the dimly lit room. However, it is not in the chapel itself where visitors become aware of the true horror of the western front. The reality becomes clear when visitors walk out the exit along a path of windows at the base of the building. Each window opens onto a chamber of bones. The windows, the chambers, and the bones seem endless. It is here that visitors get a real sense that 130,000 soldiers are buried in one mass grave.

Historians speak of a generation in Great Britain and France that was lost in the war. The numbers are almost beyond under-standing. Of the 17 million French and British troops who served on the western front, half were killed, wounded, or taken prisoner. France, in one six-month period, lost more men than the United States would lose in battle in the entire twentieth century. Over the course

The Douaumont Ossuary houses the remains of nearly 130,000 unknown soldiers. It stands in the middle of a cemetery of named casualties from the battle at Verdun, France.

of the war, it is estimated that France lost more than one-tenth of its population.

More than 900,000 soldiers and sailors died from Great Britain and other countries of the British Empire, such as Canada and Australia. One battle, at Verdun, France, lasted three hundred days. About 1 million soldiers were killed or wounded at Verdun, including the 130,000 unknown dead buried at Douaumont. French war widows numbered 650,000 by the end of the war. Great Britain had 250,000 amputees who came home by the end of the war. This was a war fought on a scale never known before that time.

THE STALEMATE

French soldiers wait in the trenches during the winter of 1917. Soldiers in the trenches had to be on constant lookout for enemy troops. The soldiers spent much of their time waiting for something to happen.

Before the United States entered the war, the armies of the Allies and the Central powers dug themselves into the ground in a series of connecting trenches. These were used as defensive positions for the soldiers.

The trenches became increasingly complex as time went on. They often included wooden huts and support beams. This made it harder for either side to attack.

The area between the trenches was lined with barbed wire and surrounded by explosives. It was known as no-man's-land. Soldiers would be sent out at night to avoid detection. They went on missions to cut the wire or perhaps to attack the enemy's trenches. Soldiers on both sides dreaded orders to "go over the top" (move out of their trenches). No one wanted to leave the shelter and protection of the trenches.

At the same time, however, both sides were frustrated with the stalemate. The Battle of the Somme had been the largest effort made by the British and French to drive the Germans from their trenches and move the battle line forward. But it had not broken the stalemate. Diary after diary and letter after letter record the horror of the fighting on the western front. One French soldier, Christian Mallett, called it "the zone of Hell. There is no word, sound or colour that can give an idea of it."

Others described the nightmare with subtle humor. Lionel Sotheby, a Welsh officer, wrote to his mother. He requested that she send him new eating supplies because "a shell [explosive] buried all my cooking & eating utensils just before my lunch the other day." He wrote to an aunt and uncle and described the death of his captain in grisly detail. However, going into battle, he wrote his father that the soldiers were "all cheerful & full of hope." Two days later, Sotheby died in the battle at Loos. He continued to lead his men even after he was wounded, "until a grenade struck him and killed him."

The diary of British soldier Jack Giffard tells another disturbing story. Jack was wounded early in the war (September 1914) when the rest of his crew were killed in an attack by German troops. He himself was wounded in the left leg, right arm, back, hip, and head. He was hit again in the right leg while hiding behind a haystack. In spite of his scary situation, he could be grateful that when "some of the stacks began to catch fire . . . ours did not."

On his way to a hospital, Giffard thought his ordeal was over. Then the ambulance he was in was captured by the Germans. He became a prisoner. Finally, the area where he was being held was retaken by the French and he was sent home to Britain. He never fought again, and he lived a long life, filled with pain from the wounds he received. Sadly, Jack's twin brother, Bob, was killed in action on October 31, 1914. Another brother died the following year, and one more brother was killed near the end of the war. A fourth brother also served and survived.

The war left millions with sad stories. Vera Brittain was a British woman who served as a nurse during the war. Her fiancé, Roland Leighton, died in December 1915. Then two of her brother's friends died from combat wounds in 1917. Finally, her brother was killed the following year. Her letters are a touching account of her experience. Vera wrote of her need to work as a nurse. The only way she could handle her own suffering was "by alleviating even if it is only a lit- tle . . . the suffering of this unhappy stricken world."

No End in Sight

Going across the barbed-wired no-man's-land was not the only hor- ror wearing down the Allies. The soldiers began to realize there was no end in sight. British officer I. L. Read summed up the feelings as the war entered its third year: "Sheer exhaustion was slowly gaining the upper hand with us. Continual shelling, the constant necessity of removing debris, and deepening our miserable defences." He went on to list the reasons that they were gloomy. They included sleepless nights, no hot meals or drinks, no way to light fires and keep warm, nasty water, and a lack of cigarettes and tobacco.

British captain J. I. Cohen wrote to a friend about life in the trenches, "This horrible country is made of mud, water and dead Germans." Another British officer was Captain Ulick Burke. He wrote of "the wet sogging through your boots. In many cases your toes nearly rotted off in your boots." Burke noted that more soldiers were disabled from trench foot (a fungal disease caused by constant con-

tact with water) than from actual wounds in battle. Once the war had reached a stalemate in 1917, diseases such as dysentery and pneumonia were killing more soldiers than bullets were.

A frostbitten British soldier picks at his meal in the trenches. The trench system was vital to both sides in protecting soldiers. But life in the trenches was dirty, cold, and miserable.

The men in the trenches knew that if they stayed there long enough, they would probably die.

French soldier George Connes found the trenches awful. He actually preferred spending the rest of the war in a prison camp. In his memoir, he wrote about the day he was captured by the Germans. "I welcome June 1, 1916, the most beautiful day in my life! I won't die, I won't be killed anymore; I have totally done my duty . . . and death has passed me by." His memoir details a life much easier than the one he had led in the trenches. His most serious problems were boredom and getting along with his fellow prisoners.

In the memoirs, letters, and diaries of the British and French troops fighting in the trenches, the most common theme is despair. It seemed that no one really believed he would ever go home or the war would ever end. A French soldier, Antoine Redier, wrote: "Trench warfare has condemned us all to the work of digging." He complained that the war "is taking us back to the age of the cave-dwellers." It's easy to understand why the Allies wanted the United States to enter the war.

THE AMERICANS WHO WOULDN'T WAIT

From the time the war began, Americans were divided over whether the United States should enter the fight. The government wanted to stay neutral in the first years of war. Some Americans decided not to wait for the government to act. They traveled to Europe on their own to join the Allies. Some went to fight in battle. Others went to provide medical care to the wounded.

Edwin Austin Abbey was one such man. In 1915 he joined a Canadian regiment, disgusted that "the country has made evident only one determination, that of avoiding the issue as long as possible." By 1916 Abbey was fighting in the trenches. He wrote of his excitement when the United States finally declared war.

Abbey also wrote a letter to be sent home if he did not return from an attack. Four days later, Abbey was killed at Vimy Ridge, France. He became one of the first Americans to die in the declared war. In that last letter home, he wrote proudly that he was going into battle "with a light heart and a determination to fight against evil, for God and humanity." He would "give my life gladly if it is asked," he wrote, "fighting for our dear flag, as thousands of Americans have before us in the cause of Liberty."

A Man without a Country

Because the United States was neutral, Americans who signed up with a foreign army took the chance of losing their citizenship. American Frederick Libby enlisted in the Canadian army and served in the trenches. Then he joined the British Royal Flying Corps as a pilot. He

shot down twenty-four German war planes and was awarded the British Military Cross by King George V.

At one point, the U.S. government said that all Americans serving with the Canadian forces "should quit or lose their American citizenship." Frederick Libby

Frederick Libby was one of many Americans who felt a need to serve in the war in Europe before the U.S. government officially declared war.

faced a choice. He was grateful that "the Canadian army agreed to release every American who wished to be released," but he decided to stay. Once the United States declared war, this honored pilot was asked to return and help develop a U.S. air corps. He would be promoted to major, and he would be given back his U.S. citizenship. It was an offer he accepted, but not without regret. "I should be awfully bucked up and happy, which isn't the way I feel. . . . It seems like I am leaving my best friends."

Another American, Edmond C. C. Genet, deserted (left without permission) from the U.S. Navy and joined French forces. He became a pilot in the Lafayette Escadrille Flying Corps. He wrote home to his brother from the trenches in January 1916 about his surprise at finding "quite a number of American fellows" fighting in his regiment. A year later, the consequences of his choices were bothering him. He didn't regret the decision. But he was concerned that it would take a presidential pardon for him to get his U.S. citizenship back. "I'm practically a man without a country," he wrote.

When the United States declared war, Genet wrote about how proud he was of his country and that he was already fighting in its name, even if "I did desert my country's service to be here." With the help of the French War Office, he immediately began the process of getting his citizenship reinstated. He would never know the result. On April 16, 1917, his plane was hit by antiaircraft fire and crashed. After his death, his mother was told that his navy records indicated he had died for his country.

Medical Personnel
Meanwhile, other Americans went to war to provide medical care to British and French soldiers. Medical care was something that Americans could provide without being punished by the U.S. government.

Daniel Sargent became part of a U.S. ambulance corps. He expressed a common attitude among medical personnel, "There was a lot of propaganda about the wickedness of the Germans. I wanted to do something." Sargent became part of the war even before he reached France when his boat was hit by a torpedo. His family was mistakenly informed that he had not survived the attack. When he finally arrived to take up his duties, everyone was relieved that he had survived.

Marie Speakman was working with the War Relief Committee in Wilmington, Delaware. Her husband was a dentist and facial surgeon. He traveled to France in June 1915. A group of dentists, all former classmates from the University of Pennsylvania, formed their own unit. They sailed to France, all at their own expense, to help the doctors care for the wounded. Dr. Speakman details the care of troops who had their chins "entirely

Many Americans served on hospital ships such as this Red Cross ship stationed in Falmouth Harbor, Great Britain. Falmouth is on the southern coast of Britain across the English Channel from France.

blown away; the teeth all gone and the nose missing." He was proud of what he and his fellow dentists accomplished with these patients.

Dr. Speakman returned to the United States in November to give lectures and raise money for the relief efforts. When he went back to France, Marie Speakman went with him. She was amazed by the needs of the troops and civilians there and by the gratefulness of those she met. Dr. Speakman wrote that he felt "sorry for the self-contented man who stays at home . . . without doing his share." For both of the Speakmans, supporting the war was a responsibility for every citizen, "working as a keen, alive member of a large national family."

Activists

The United States might not have been at war, but for many Americans, their country was not at peace either. As time passed, the situation in Europe continued to get worse. Activists became more vocal in their support for the Allies. They demanded U.S. involvement.

Those who were against entering the war were just as vocal. Much of the opposition came from Americans of German ancestry. Native German Minne Allen was living with her American husband in Ann Arbor, Michigan. She spoke out against entering the war. Allen was angry at U.S. political leaders, but she mostly criticized people whom she thought were traitors among the German American community. "It pains me more than I can say," she wrote to her mother, "that the immigrants from our beloved fatherland see their German-American being in terms of their own egotistical interests, not in terms of the homeland itself."

Many Americans who were against the war were pleased when President Woodrow Wilson ran for reelection in 1916. His slogan was, "He kept us out of war." They hoped that the United States would stay neutral for the rest of the war. Wilson was determined to do so, at least until he believed it was right for the United States to get involved. But it was a German decision, not an American one, that would finally force the United States to join the Allies. German submarines attacked the ships of neutral nations, including the United States. This act sent the American Doughboys off to war.

THE ROAD TO WAR

The submarine was a fairly new military weapon. A few had been used before World War I, but the Germans were the first to make them useful weapons. The Germans used their fleet of *Unterseeboot* (undersea boats), or U-boats, to attack commercial shipping in the Atlantic. They wanted to cut off the flow of supplies to Great Britain and France from the United States and Canada. This would reduce the threat to Germany. Early in the war, the new boats were not a large factor in giving Germany an edge

A damaged German U-boat surfaces off the Danish coast. U-boats became a symbol of the German military for members of the Allied forces.

THE WORLD WAR I LOOK

After the first months of the war, it was clear that the soldiers in the trenches needed head gear. A helmet was designed in 1915 by John L. Brodie for the British army. The helmet was a far cry from the modern lightweight Kevlar helmet. It was a metal, dome-shaped, uncomfortable-looking hat with a leather liner and chinstrap. The World War I helmet (called the M1917 by the military) had a clear purpose—to protect the top of the wearer's head from bullets and shrapnel.

This same model was chosen for the U.S. Army. The U.S. government bought 400,000 of them from the British and then began making their own version. This unique helmet always seems to be the main image of the World War I Doughboy. Compared to the felt hats of earlier wars, the helmet protected from more than just the weather. However, it was uncomfortable to wear and did not provide as much protection as helmets that were made later.

The Doughboys wore another hat when they were not in the field. It was a style that some state police officers still wear. With a large, stiff flat brim, this brown felt hat protected soldiers from the weather. It was part of the gear they carried, along with their blanket roll, a small entrenching shovel, a canteen, a haversack (a backpack worn over one shoulder), and a rifle.

over the Allies. As the war continued, however, the Germans became better at harming the supply pipeline.

During that time, a German submarine sank the *Lusitania*, a British ship. More than one thousand people died, including more than one hundred U.S. citizens. The attack was not the first that had

This painting from 1915 shows the British ocean liner *Lusitania* being hit by a torpedo. The passenger ship was sailing off the coast of Ireland when it was attacked by a German U-boat.

involved Americans. It followed others with less loss of life, including attacks on ships sailing under the U.S. flag. The United States reacted immediately to the *Lusitania* attack. The U.S. government warned the German government that "the lives of non-combatants, whether they be of neutral citizenship or citizens of one of the nations at war, cannot lawfully or rightfully be put in jeopardy." For more than a year, there was an uneasy peace on the seas.

However, in early 1917, the German government said that it would begin attacking all shipping on the seas in certain areas. The United States responded by breaking off ties with Germany. At the same time, President Wilson told Congress and the American people that he still hoped to avoid war. "We do not desire any hostile conflict with the Imperial Government. We are the sincere friends of the German people."

Historians disagree about Germany's actions at this time. Many believe that the United States did not stay strictly neutral as it was supposed to. They say the Germans were just recognizing that a state of war already existed. Most historians judge that the German government was too confident. Its leaders believed they were close to winning. The Germans thought that the entry of the Americans would come too late to be a factor and that total control of the seas would ensure Germany's victory. Achieving that control was worth the risk of U.S. involvement.

Whatever the reasons, Germany decided to attack all ships bringing supplies of any kind to its enemies. This included ships sailing under the flag of neutral nations. On April 2, 1917, President Wilson told Congress that "the recent course of the Imperial German Government . . . [is] in fact nothing less than war against the Government and people of the United States." This led to the United States' declaring war on April 6.

In words that would echo through the rest of the century and into the next, President Wilson stated a noble reason for war: "The world must be made safe for democracy." The United States, a free and democratic country, would join the other constitutional democracies,

> "The world must be made safe for democracy."
> —President Woodrow Wilson, 1917

Britain and France. Together they would defeat the empires that had broken world peace and bring democracy to their citizens. This was considered a noble goal and one that Americans could support.

The entry of the United States into the European conflict turned this war into a world war. It would be called the Great War until time showed that there could be bigger ones. The war gave Americans a way to "dedicate our lives and our fortunes, everything that we are and everything that we have, with the pride of those who know the day has come when America is privileged to spend her blood and her might for the principles that gave her birth." The wait was over.

> ❝Anyhow, I thought, I can go to France and grow up with the war."
>
> —Martin J. Hogan, 1919, in reference to his experience during World War I

CHAPTER THREE

AMERICA FINALLY GOES TO WAR

The United States was not ready for war when it joined the fight in 1917. The strange story of Alexander W. Moffatt shows just how unprepared the country was. Moffatt joined the navy as a machinist's mate (a sailor whose job is to maintain the engines on a ship). The day he was to report for duty, a friend in New York named Len Breed got in touch with him. Breed told Moffatt he had heard that people could join the navy by providing their own yacht. They would lease the yacht to the navy for one dollar a year. "Then you sail around New York harbor all day and go ashore every night," said Breed.

The next day, Moffatt and Breed bought an 80-foot yacht named the *Tamarack*. Moffatt reported to the officer in charge of accepting their ship into the navy. After some simple questions, Moffatt was accepted and sworn in.

Several days later, Moffatt was called back. Moffatt's commander told him that he would be made an officer and captain of the *Tamarack*. Moffatt replied, "But I have no training whatever to be an officer." That didn't change the commander's mind. Moffatt's adventure as captain of the *Tamarack* began the next month. Little did he know that this job would lead him to other adventures as captain of a submarine chaser. And he did not spend the rest of the war in New York Harbor after all.

THE DRAFT

The United States had never been part of a world war before. All the fighting would take place several thousand miles from its shores. The challenges of moving hundreds of thousands of troops and all of their gear to Europe were hard enough. The threat of German submarines only added to the Americans' fears.

The task of organizing, training, and supplying an army was greater than anything the country had done in the past. The United States entered the war with an army of only about 300,000 trained soldiers. Of those, 175,000 were in the National Guard, not the regular army. All told, about 4 million Americans served in the army during World War I. Another 800,000 were in other services, such as the navy or the air corps. Most of them had no military training.

To build an army, Congress passed the Selective Service Act in May 1917. It required all men from twenty-one to thirty years of age to sign up with their local draft board. More than 9 million men signed up on the first day of the draft (June 5). A national lottery took place on July 20 to choose the first group of draftees, or men

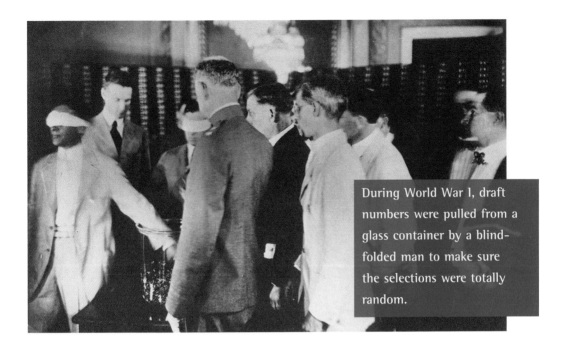

During World War 1, draft numbers were pulled from a glass container by a blindfolded man to make sure the selections were totally random.

who would have to serve. Later, the ages for the draft were changed to include men aged eighteen to thirty-five.

In all, almost 25 million men signed up. Many men volunteered rather than wait for the draft. Volunteering gave them a better chance to choose what they would be doing in the armed forces. However, two-thirds of the American Expeditionary Force (AEF)—the force that served in Europe—were draftees. The only men who did not have to register were the Native Americans who had not yet been granted U.S. citizenship.

Draft law did not care about race. Unlike in the Civil War, African Americans were treated "equally" by these laws. However, according to a report by historian W. Alison Sweeney published shortly after the war ended, "a much higher percentage of Negroes were accepted for service than of white men," and they were placed in separate military units.

Almost 3 million African Americans served in the army. They "were a source of terror to the Germans throughout the war, and objects of

These men were members of the all-African American 369th Infantry Regiment. During World War I, African Americans served in separate military units.

great curiosity to the German people afterwards." It is not known why the Germans were so scared of the African American troops. But the German government pushed African American soldiers to desert or refuse to fight. Copies of German propaganda flyers are in the National Archives. They ask why African Americans would want to fight for a country that didn't grant them the same rights as white citizens.

SIGNING UP

Native Americans who did not hold citizenship (about one-third of the Native American population) did not have to sign up for the draft. But this did not keep Native Americans from joining the fight. An estimated twelve thousand Native Americans served in the army.

Unlike African American soldiers, Native American soldiers served in army units with white Americans.

One historian notes that casualties among Native American soldiers were much higher than among other groups. Native Americans had a casualty rate of about 5 percent. U.S. soldiers had a total casualty rate of 2.7 percent. This difference may have been because Native American soldiers often served as scouts. The use of Native American scouts was already an old tradition in the U.S. Army. It was not surprising that the practice continued during World War I.

Being a scout was a risky job. Scouts were alone or in very small patrols. Their job was to move beyond the front lines. Sometimes they even went behind enemy lines to learn more about the enemy's plans.

Young people were also eager to join the war. One group of soldiers that reported for duty had five men under eighteen who had sneaked in. One of them, Martin J. Hogan, was seventeen when he

SCIENCE COMES TO MILITARY TRAINING

Shortly before World War I, a new intelligence test was created by French psychologist Alfred Binet. A Stanford University professor named Lewis Terman adapted it for use in the United States. With the start of the war, scientists saw a chance to try it out among the draftees. The army used the test as a tool for assigning soldiers to jobs within the army. The decision was controversial. The results of the tests showed great differences among racial and ethnic groups.

Eventually, the testers realized that the results were too simplistic. They were not a good measure of the soldiers' abilities. The use of the Stanford-Binet IQ Test, however, did begin a long history of testing to find out where people fit within a group on certain test criteria. This kind of testing still stirs up a lot of debates, especially when it is used in schools.

joined. Hogan explained his actions this way: "The call for men was urgent enough to justify me in camouflaging my age by one year. Anyhow, I thought, I can go to France and grow up with the war." He remembered the first sergeant of his unit inspecting them for the first time. He commented that he had gotten "a Boy Scout outfit."

Many of the Doughboys signed up after serious thought. "There was only one thing for all of us to do, and we did it," wrote Warren Jackson of his decision to be a marine for up to four years. However, he also said that he and the others felt a great deal of pressure. He said they "were afraid not to sign."

Traveling Overseas

When it came to actually going overseas, the trip was a great experience for some. For others it was an ordeal. This depended largely on how lucky the troops were with their ship assignments. For Charles MacArthur, it was an ordeal. "We reached France just like ordinary soldiers, packed in the coal bunkers of the *President Lincoln* so tight that you couldn't talk without biting off somebody's ear."

Conditions on army ships, such as the one shown here, were extremely cramped.

Stillman Westbrook had the opposite experience. Westbrook was a member of a Connecticut National Guard unit that was called up as a machine-gun battalion. He wrote home that he was traveling "in the luxurious smoking room of a . . . trans-Atlantic liner, a steward at my elbow ready and willing to render any service."

Some of this was because Charles MacArthur was a private while Westbrook was an officer. But most of it was the luck of which ship they were assigned to. Officers always had better quarters on board ship than their men, but few had the luxury that Westbrook did.

Corporal Louis Ranlett found that leaving for war was quite moving. He wrote of watching Staten Island in the sunset. He was "spellbound by the wonder of the fact that here I was, actually going to war."

Ray Herring also watched carefully as the Statue of Liberty faded away. He thought of "its connection with France and Revolutionary America." As soon as they were fully out to sea, however, his interests turned from patriotism to survival. He joined the others in looking for any sign of submarines. "Every little whitecap appeared suspicious," he wrote. It was the greatest fear for the men on the ships.

TORPEDOES

Although few ships were ever in danger, the fear of enemy submarines was real. One British troopship, the *Tuscania*, was sunk by the Germans. It was torpedoed on February 5, 1918, while carrying more than two thousand U.S. troops. One-tenth of them died when the boat sank several hours after being hit.

Survivor Everett Harphan wrote that the torpedo's explosion "shook the great liner from bow to stern as if she was a toy." He remembered the frightened rush to get on deck and into lifeboats. He also remembered the time spent in the lifeboats. They were "tossed like a chip in ice-cold water up to our knees."

Survivors from the *Tuscania* share a meal on February 15, 1918.

In total, four other navy transport ships were torpedoed, but these attacks occurred while they were on their way home. Some of them were carrying wounded troops. Two of those sunk, but the other two were able to make it into port to be fixed.

The *President Lincoln* sank on May 31, 1918, after being hit by two torpedoes. The survivors managed to keep their lifeboats together until they were rescued the following night. As a result, out of the 700 men aboard, only 26 were lost.

In spite of any fears and discomforts, going "over there" was a great adventure for these troops. Many had never seen the ocean, and now they were traveling across it to Europe. For most, this would be the longest trip of their lives. They also knew that it was an adventure from which they might not return.

The troops had no illusions about this war. They had read enough of the news accounts to know that what they would find there was a nightmare. William Langer wrote, "Here was our one great chance for excitement and risk. We could not afford to pass it up."

CHAPTER FOUR

FITTING IN "OVER THERE"

British officer Edward Heron-Allen was excited when the Americans finally announced they were entering the war on the side of the Allies. Heron-Allen knew that the Allies needed help badly. The decisions made by the United States soon after declaring war made him even more hopeful. "They do seem to be profiting from our mistakes," he wrote, "dealing with the war-factors that we have proved ourselves absolutely powerless to deal with." The U.S. government's decision to enter the war was an opportunity to provide more troops to the Allies. It also led to improving the tactics and strategies that the Allies had been using.

Before the Americans joined the fight, the war effort had

become stagnant. The system of trenches on the western front had become a killing field. No one could see a solution. The Americans did not enter the war to add more men to the trenches. Instead, they were determined to shake up the entire line. They planned to fight the war on open ground. The Doughboys were going to change the way the war was fought.

HOSTILITY AND MISUNDERSTANDINGS

The Americans, the French, and the British would fight the war together. But this did not mean that they would all like one another. William Langer was "truly shocked by the hostility of the average American Doughboy toward the 'Limey' [nickname for the British]." Ray Herring was one of those who was hostile. He felt that "the English never did anything, had their fighting done for them."

The feelings of the British about the Americans were just as negative. Captain Gibbs of the Welsh Guards wrote to his mother, "The Americans are splendid fighters, but their officers aren't much good at present: much too sympathetic with their men, and inclined to invite instead of order the men to do things."

Relations with the French were not always friendly either, in spite of the "Lafayette, we are here" sentiment. The U.S. soldiers in Europe were not stationed in military housing. They were divided up and stationed in French towns as they began their training. Within the towns, they lived in French barns and sometimes in French homes.

Unfortunately, few Americans spoke French. Their knowledge of French customs and manners was also poor. Doughboy Ray Herring was one of the few who was more willing to fight alongside French troops than alongside the British. He noted, "because things in France might be different . . . [they were] not necessarily . . . wrong."

WHAT'S IN A NAME?

The British called the French Frogs, possibly because French cuisine includes frogs' legs. Doughboys also called the French the poilus—a French word meaning "hairy." Poilus is also a French slang term for "tough."

The British were called Limeys. The nickname comes from British naval history. British sailors carried limes on board naval ships. The men ate the limes to prevent scurvy, a disease caused by lack of vitamin C. Fruit such as limes is a good source of the vitamin.

English speakers sometimes referred to the Germans as Fritz or Dutch or Hun. But most often they were called the Boche or Boches. This was a French nickname that comes from the word *caboche*, which means "cabbage." It is also a French term for a *blockhead*, someone who is obstinate or stubborn.

The Europeans called the Americans Sammies. This word comes from the term *Uncle Sam*. They also called the Americans Doughboys. The word *Doughboy* has a long history as a name for U.S. troops. It was first used in the Mexican War in 1846. The United States fought against Mexico for the control of territory in the Southwest. U.S. cavalrymen, who rode on horses, called the foot soldiers, or infantry, doughboys. After long marches over dusty land, the soldiers looked like they were covered in flour (or dough).

Many other theories explain the origins of the nickname Doughboys. Some think the use of the name came from the fact that the U.S. troops were well paid. They had a lot of "dough," an English slang word for *money*. Others say the word comes from "fried dough" (the early doughnut), which the American troops loved to eat. Over time, the term *Doughboy* came to mean all the officers and troops who made up the American Expeditionary Force.

The nicknames were mostly harmless. They were an easy way to refer to troops of different nationalities. However, U.S. troops did not like to be called Sammies. They preferred to be called Doughboys.

Some of the misunderstandings between U.S. soldiers and French citizens were humorous. Lieutenant C. C. Van Gooding watched one of the soldiers talking with a farmer. The soldier was trying to buy a chicken. Gooding said the soldier was "jumping up and down waving his arms and crowing like a rooster."

European commanders had different opinions on how to best use the new U.S. troops. Many U.S. soldiers' memoirs explain that the Europeans met them with mixed feelings: "Welcome, now what should we do with you?"

However, Winston Churchill (who later became British prime minister)

U.S. troops get off an army ship in Liverpool, England *(below)*. Most of the men and women serving in the army had never been out of the United States. This led to some cultural misunderstandings between troops from different countries.

explained best what the American Expeditionary Force meant to the Allies. He described the arriving Americans as a "seemingly inexhaustible flood of gleaming youth in its first maturity of health and vigour... half trained, half organized... [ready] to buy their experience."

Even with all the problems, the armies cooperated well with one another. Perhaps this was because they knew they had to cooperate to defeat the Germans. Once the Americans actually fought in battle, they commented on how much they liked the British and French troops. They also greatly respected their courage.

> **Americans are a "seemingly inexhaustible flood of gleaming youth in its first maturity of health and vigour... half trained, half organized... [ready] to buy their experience."**
>
> **—Winston Churchill, 1927, in reference to World War I**

PREPARING FOR BATTLE

The British and French armies believed that over time they had gained a lot of experience in fighting the war. Therefore, they felt that the new and inexperienced U.S. troops should be trained and led by British or French officers. Plus, many people believed the U.S. Army was not strong. One modern historian notes that they were "ranked sixteenth, just behind Portugal."

Debates over who should command U.S. troops caused tension. U.S. major general Hunter Liggett bluntly described the Allies' attitude about American command of U.S. troops. "From the day of our declaration of war until less than a month prior to the Armistice, our Allies endeavoured—by argument, cajolery, flattery... by social, political

TRAINING TO BE PRESIDENT

In 1917 Harry Truman went to fight in the Great War. He was thirty-three years old and had never married. He had been working on his family farm in Kansas and spent some time in the National Guard. When the war began, Truman had some military experience. Although he was not subject to the draft because of his age, he signed up because he wanted to fight.

When Truman's local guard unit was brought into the army, he was a first lieutenant for Battery F of the 129th Field Artillery Unit. By April 1918, he arrived in France for advanced weapons training. He was then promoted to captain and given command of Battery D. The unit was involved in the heavy fighting of Saint-Mihiel and the Meuse offensive in France. Truman was praised for his abilities as a military leader.

When the war ended, Truman came home with millions of other Doughboys. A popular song of the time was called "How 'Ya Gonna Keep 'Em Down on the Farm After They've Seen Paree [Paris]." The song was very true for Truman. The farmboy did not return to the farm. He entered public service after winning election as an administrative judge. He went on to become a U.S. senator in 1934, and then he was elected vice president in 1944. President Franklin D. Roosevelt died in 1945. The farmboy from Kansas who went off to the Great War became president of the United States.

and military pressure . . . to sway the United States from its insistence on an independent American Army."

U.S. commanders had observed the Allies' tactics and saw how ineffective they were. The Allies needed fresh troops, and they also badly needed fresh strategy. General John J. Pershing, commander of all the troops in the American Expeditionary Force, reminded the Allies, "We all desire the same thing, but our means of attaining it are different from yours. America declared war independently of the Allies. . . . [T]he morale of our soldiers depends upon their fighting under our own flag."

The Americans did not want to spend their time in the trenches. They were not interested in filling in for British and French troops who had been killed. They were going to take the offensive in the war. Lieutenant Quincy Mills noted in a letter to his mother, "The Poilus [French] think that the Americans incline to rashness in always picking on the Boche [German] and keeping him stirred up continually, but that is a good trait."

> "No more ham or eggs or grapefruit when the bugle blows for chow. No more apple pie or dumplings, for we're in the army now..."
>
> —*Stars and Stripes*, 1918

CHAPTER FIVE

THE DAILY LIFE OF THE TROOPS

"[Lice] don't make big bites like fleas; they just sit in your underclothes or else crawl around and nibble and tickle a bit," William Upson said years after the war. This funny description of lice is probably not how Upson would have described his experiences when he was actually living as a soldier in France. At the time, the lice problem would have seemed much less amusing.

The troops' lives were filled with little nagging things that reminded them every day that they would much rather be home. The lives of the Doughboys were filled with complaints. They complained mostly about lice, drilling and marching, food, mail, and their superior officers.

LITTLE PETS

Lice were a serious problem for the troops. Lice are brought up in just about every account of the war. These little bugs were a nuisance to both the infantry and the officers who led it. As in earlier wars, there was really no getting away from the lice. When the 149th Artillery of the United States was ordered to move into some shacks that had recently held German prisoners, the troops spent three days trying to get rid of the lice in order to make their quarters livable.

Those in the trenches fared even worse. U.S. lieutenant Quincy Mills wrote to his mother about his soldiers' "little pets." He was quite happy to have so far escaped this "souvenir of the trenches." Others wrote home about how good it felt when they were moved back from the trenches. They had the chance to clean up and change into clean clothing.

One historian wrote about the morale of the troops. He said: "The men were in good spirits, though there was the usual grumbling; they would not have been soldiers if they had not grumbled." Most of the grumbling was expected.

DRILLS, DRILLS, AND MORE DRILLS

The Doughboys complained about the amount of time they spent drilling and learning to fight. There were drills in advancing and retreating, close-order drills in how to use a bayonet, drills in throwing hand grenades and, most important, drills in how to use gas masks. (Poison gas attacks had become a battle tactic for both sides of the conflict. The gas could kill within seconds, so this was the one drill that the troops respected.) "Drills, drills, drills, drills," grumbled Charles MacArthur.

The Doughboys started drills even before they were deployed to Europe. These troops are practicing trench attacks in a training camp in the United States.

It was important for the troops to learn how to fight as organized units. But Warren Jackson thought the long hours of drill were extreme. He echoed a complaint common to troops of earlier wars. He noted that officers, instead of simply training troops to fight effectively, trained as if they would have to "parade in Washington."

BAD FOOD AND GOOD NEWS

Food has always been the favorite topic of complaint by troops. Ray Herring stated his honest opinion about the food. He noted that although it was "the soldiers' right and privilege" to complain about the food they were served, it was "not counting the potatoes ... fairly good."

Not all the troops would agree. Warren Jackson wrote of a time when his unit was under fire and food could not get to them. When they did receive some, it was "French hard bread and French corned beef, known as monkey meat."

An issue of the army newspaper *Stars and Stripes* included this witty description of army food: "No more ham or eggs or grapefruit when the bugle blows for chow. No more apple pie or dumplings, for we're in the army now; and they feed us beans for breakfast, and at noon we have 'em, too; while at night they fill our tummies with a good old army stew."

Stars and Stripes was created to give the soldiers some idea of what was going on around them—how the war was going, what was

This is the front page of the army newspaper *Stars and Stripes* for June 28, 1918. *Stars and Stripes* was first published during the Civil War (1861–1865). The paper resumed publication during World War 1 and again during World War 11. Since World War 11, it has been published continuously for U.S. military personnel around the world.

happening in the United States, and so on. Army leaders believed the paper would help lessen the effects of rumors. Published especially for the American Expeditionary Force, it became an institution.

The eight-page newspaper was a combination of humor, official policy, propaganda against the enemy, advice, and how-to columns. *Stars and Stripes* tackled a wide range of issues, from dental care to preventing trench foot. It also included general gossip. The paper served as an outlet for the troops' complaints and helped boost the troops' morale.

LOST MAIL

One of the most frustrating issues for the troops was how long it took for them to receive their mail. Major Speakman thought the failures of the postal system were "more than anything else . . . responsible for the feeling of homesickness."

Reading the accounts of the war, it seems that a good portion of the mail, perhaps more than half, never reached its destination. Many troops started numbering their letters home and had those writing to them do the same. This gave them an idea of what was getting lost along the way.

Mail was also censored. One of the jobs of the lieutenant of each unit was to censor the letters written by his men to their families and friends back home. This was necessary to ensure that if the letters got into enemy hands, they would not reveal anything important about the Allies' strategies and plans.

ALCOHOL USE

Alcohol use was an issue between the troops and their officers. Daniel Poling was the official representative of the United Society of Christian Endeavor. He traveled to the western front to report on the general morals of the U.S. troops. "No nation has ever been rep-resented by cleaner-living men than those who wear the uniform of the United States," he wrote in his report.

Many officers dealing with day-to-day problems among the troops might not have agreed. Troops who were brought back from the front for rest and a break from the fighting often went looking for something to do. This included drinking alcohol.

At the time, temperance was a major social issue in the United States. Excessive drinking was seen as a social danger. Many feared that the troops would come home as chronic drinkers. In 1917 Congress passed the Eighteenth Amendment to the Constitution, also called Prohibition. It banned the sale and use of alcohol in the United States. (Prohibition was in effect from 1920 until it was can-celed in 1933.)

Commanders of the American Expeditionary Force tried to enforce the same rules on the troops serving in France. *Stars and Stripes* reported the promulgation of General Order 213. This was aimed at "the suppression of the drink evil."

FORBIDDEN MEETINGS

The troops also engaged in another activity that earned the wrath of their commanders. As in previous wars, there were documented accounts of troops from both sides calling their own short truce and getting to know their enemy. This was always strongly discouraged by commanders on both sides. It was believed that getting to know the enemy might make the troops less likely to follow orders to kill them or, at least, more reluctant to do so.

German soldier Ernst Jünger describes one of the times when the troops met in no-man's-land between the trenches. They had "a lively traffic and exchange going on in schnaps, cigarettes, uniform buttons."

THOSE WHO DID NOT DESERT

Desertion (leaving one's military duty without permission) was a serious problem at some points in U.S. history. This was especially true in the Revolutionary and Civil wars. Desertion was punishable by death under military law. But no one was sentenced to die for this crime in World War I. In fact, World War I stands out as the war with the lowest desertion rates in U.S. history.

Of the more than 4 million troops in the American Expeditionary Force, only about 2,600 were convicted of desertion (out of about 5,500 accused of the crime). This was less than 1 percent of the military. One theory for the low desertion rates is based on the fact that these rates increase as wars drag on for years. U.S. troops were officially involved in World War I for only sixteen months, so the period of military service was limited. Plus, troops were far from home. Desertion might have left them in a foreign land with nowhere to go.

Military police—soldiers assigned to police the troops—were kept busy in France. But the crimes they dealt with rarely carried the death penalty. When the pressures of war eased, military police found themselves handling complaints of drunkenness or fighting. They also had to settle disputes among the troops and the French villagers.

Historians have noticed that disciplinary issues among the Doughboys became worse in the months after the war ended. As the soldiers waited to be sent back to the United States, they became bored and unruly. Troops who are fighting an enemy have less free time to get into fights among themselves.

Jünger was an officer who had been wounded six times and thus had much reason to hate the enemy. However, he later observed that he always distinguished between actual battle conditions in which the enemy needed to be seen as an enemy and other times when he would "honour him as a man according to his courage."

Commanders did not want the troops seeing humanity in the enemy. These meetings were strongly forbidden.

This was yet another gripe the troops felt about their lives. Life had become a world of order and drill. There were no more choices of food or drink or how to spend free time.

In addition, soldiers often felt cut off from family and friends at home. To the troops, it seemed unnecessary. To the officers and the army command, strict discipline was crucial. Disciplined troops could become the fighting units needed to face the horror and hazards of war.

> "There was no breeze on the hot June nights to carry the gas away."
>
> —Carl Brannen, 1918

CHAPTER SIX

THE HAZARDS OF WAR

"We learned the world was made of mud ... abiding, clinging, sticky mud," wrote Doughboy Warren Jackson. It is hard to think of mud as a serious problem in war. However, the diaries and letters of those who were on the western front say that it was indeed one of the true hazards of the war.

The Doughboys were not as confined to the trenches as their allies had been. But they certainly spent enough of their time there to share the general western front opinion of mud. "Living three days in a muddy ditch is not conducive to cleanliness, we were simply plastered with mud from head to foot," wrote American Edwin Abbey from the western front.

The mud brought problems and general misery to the lives of the Doughboys. Living in mud with poor sanitary conditions led to disease. In an age before antibiotics, this could lead to death.

DISEASES

Disease has always traveled with the armies of the world. However, conditions in the trenches on the western front made it hard to control the wave of diseases.

When armies are on the move, they keep moving away from the waste they create. They move to cleaner conditions and relatively unspoiled areas. But the millions of men fighting in the trenches had been there for several years. The arriving Doughboys joined them, moving into those long-occupied breeding grounds for disease. Doughboy Carl Brannen wrote of the U.S. Marines at Belleau Wood, "Nearly all affected with dysentery from the scanty unfit food and polluted water."

Along with the troops, the trenches were occupied by lice, rats, frogs, and insects. The lice were responsible for a disease called

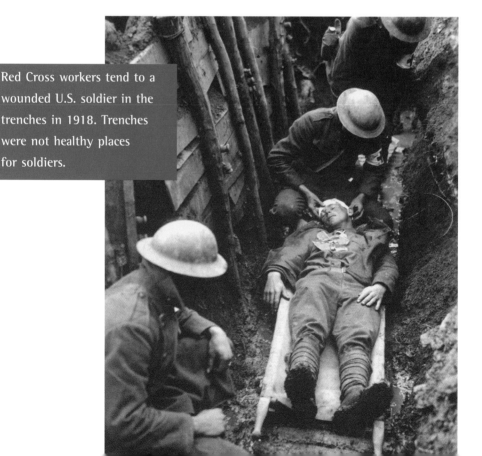

Red Cross workers tend to a wounded U.S. soldier in the trenches in 1918. Trenches were not healthy places for soldiers.

trench fever and were also carriers of the deadly typhus fever. The rats, which many say often achieved the size of cats, were everywhere. These pests alone would have caused high disease rates, as their droppings dirtied food and water supplies.

> "Nearly all affected with dysentery from the scanty unfit food and polluted water."
> —Carl Brannen, 1918

The constant presence of water was another major problem. The troops standing in the trenches in wet and cold conditions suffered from trench foot (freezing of the feet). This condition could lead to gangrene, which is when blood is cut off from a body part and the flesh decays.

Articles in *Stars and Stripes* detailed the constant nagging of the troops over the need for action to prevent disease. An article claimed trench foot was caused in part by "too infrequent changes of shoes and socks, allowing accumulations of bacteria-laden secretions."

In August 1918, the newspaper bragged about a new report. It said that the army had lost less than 3 percent of available working time from disease since it arrived in France. It said there were 131,075 cases reported and only 923 deaths. These numbers seem optimistic given the final estimates of more than 63,000 disease-related deaths among the Doughboys. But the figures do show how much effort was put into keeping the troops healthy. In fact, more than half of the deaths of Americans in World War I were from disease, rather than from battle wounds. This was a great improvement over the rates of death from disease in earlier wars.

Flu Epidemic

Just as the American Expeditionary Force became active on the battlefield, the worldwide flu epidemic of 1918 began. The great record the doctors had in keeping the troops healthy was quickly ruined as wave after wave of the Doughboys got sick. Some say that 100,000 Doughboys caught the flu, and 10 percent of them died from it.

Robert H. Zieger wrote about the 88th Division, which was made up of 18,000 men. One-third of them got the flu, resulting in 444 deaths. The same division, in battle, lost only 90 men killed or wounded. U.S. Army nurse Mary Dobson remembered that half the troops were already sick on the boats coming over from the United States. There was nothing that could be done for them without antibiotics. "It was gruesome," she wrote.

Dr. John G. Nelson was frustrated that the doctors were unable to stop the disease. "Men in apparently splendid health and perfect physical condition were suddenly desperately ill, and many of them dead in less than forty-eight hours. One week in October 1918," he wrote, "there was a series of nearly 100 'flu' and pneumonia cases of whom over 80 percent died." The epidemic was wrecking everything that the army commanders had worked for.

Chemical Warfare

Diseases were not the only hazards slowing down the troops. This modern war became associated with the chemical weapons used to fight it. "The Boches keep the town soaked with phosgene and mustard [gases]," wrote Louis Ranlett of a village where his unit was living. "And the stuff settles in all the hollows, kills the trees and grass, and spoils the water in the brook. You can't even wash in that water without getting burned."

POISON GAS

Even the names sound frightening—phosgene, chlorine, mustard gas, bromine, prussic acid. The use of poison gas was unheard of before World War I. By the end of the war, it had become one of the major elements of the conflict.

The use of chemical substances began in 1914 with the French and German use of tear gas, a nonlethal substance used to subdue the enemy. By 1915 at Ypres, Belgium, the gas attacks turned deadly. Chlorine gas shells fired by German troops covered the battlefield with a greenish yellow cloud. As the gas spread, the troops watching the approaching cloud did not know that, within seconds of breathing it, they would be choking for air and fighting for their lives.

The world was shocked by the use of poison gas. But the shock did not stop the Allies from striking back. The British quickly taught their own troops how to use gas as a weapon of war. They also came up with a way to deliver the gas through long-distance shells. As a result, the soldiers firing the gas would not feel its effects themselves.

Both sides also began to use gas masks *(below)*. The troops learned to put them on at the first sign of a chemical attack. Gas masks were heavy and uncomfortable, but they offered some protection from breathing the deadly poisons. However, they could not be worn forever. Many letters and diaries told of how the effects of the gas lingered in areas that had been attacked over and over again. It affected the water, soil, plants, trees, and animals.

Although the Germans made the most frequent use of poison gas, it was also used by the British and French as trench warfare continued. The horror of poison gas outlived the war. In 1925 the use of poison gas was formally outlawed by worldwide agreement. Yet the use of chemical and biological warfare is an issue that still troubles the world in modern times.

The Germans had made the first gas attacks in April 1915. The Allies had responded with similar weapons shortly thereafter. Chlorine gas was used first and later phosgene and then mustard gas. The mustard gas "burned out the lungs if breathed and raised huge, painful blisters on exposed skin; many were blinded by it."

Gas warfare was the terror of the western front. Doughboys, whose every memoir complained of drills, made one exception. They would drill as often as needed to avoid breathing poisonous gas. The goal was to be able to get one's gas mask in place within five seconds. However, as Ranlett noted, gas was not just something that one could wait out by wearing a gas mask until the gas went away. Chemicals had poisoned the entire region.

U.S. Marine Carl Brannen talked about the same problem. "There was no breeze on

This photograph was posed and taken to show soldiers what would happen to them if they weren't wearing their masks during a gas attack.

the hot June nights to carry the gas away. . . . [M]y nostrils stayed raw for several days. . . . [S]cratches on your body were kept irritated by the gas."

Daniel Poling was touring the front for Christian Endeavor. He was affected by the gas even though he was never in an actual gas attack. He wrote, "My lungs were sore, my throat burned, my vocal chords were affected, and I coughed deeply." He insisted that the gas was causing many other diseases not considered gas-related, including pneumonia, pleurisy, and tuberculosis. These diseases were occurring in greater numbers than expected. Chemical warfare was, he said, "a fiendish weapon of refined barbarism."

> **"My lungs were sore, my throat burned, my vocal chords were affected, and I coughed deeply."**
>
> –Daniel Poling, 1918

MECHANIZED WARFARE

In battle the Doughboys also faced the hazards of new technology. The submarine and the airplane were beginning to have an effect on the outcome of the war. Zeppelins—hydrogen-filled airships that could carry explosives and gas—were another new military development. Mechanized warfare required both sides to constantly research and develop new weapons and technology in an attempt to stay ahead of the enemy.

One of the deadliest battlefield technologies—the machine gun—was actually from a previous war. At the end of the Civil War, a new invention called the Gatling gun was used by the United States. Its barrel was turned by a crank, so the Gatling gun could fire bullets at a much higher speed than any other type of weapon. Fifty years later, the Gatling gun had been taken several steps further. The machine gun could fire more than four hundred bullets a minute. It could literally tear an enemy to pieces.

The Germans began using the machine gun early in the war. They trained special units of soldiers in its use. The British and French saw how effective it was and quickly formed their own machine-gun companies to fight alongside their foot soldiers. The American Doughboys also started using machine guns. William Langer remembered the "stuttering breathless chatter of the machine guns."

Another scary new technology of the war was a modern form of an old weapon—the flamethrower. The concept of using fire as a weapon had been around for centuries. The Germans turned it into

Machine-gun technology was new in World War 1. This U.S. soldier is in a trench aiming a British-made Lewis gun.

a modern weapon. They surprised the British and French with their *Flammenwerfer.*

The flamethrower looked like a gun, but it sent a sheet of burning oil about 50 feet from its muzzle. It was a scary weapon to face. Seeing how effective it was on the battlefield, the British quickly embraced the technology. When the Doughboys entered the war, whole units were formed whose specialty was gas warfare and the use of flamethrowers.

The tank was another technology that was refined as the war dragged on. The tank arrived on the battlefield in 1916 as a weapon to drive the Germans from their trenches. It was to take the place of the cavalry, the horse-mounted units that had been used for centuries.

Tanks did not have a great start. They were more likely to break down than to achieve a battle victory. However, they did scare the Germans, at least until they discovered that the tanks could be disabled with enough firepower. By the end of the war, tanks had become a strategic weapon for the British and French but were not used much by the Americans.

Gas warfare, machine guns, flamethrowers, and tanks—the methods of killing the enemy took a great leap forward in World War I. Each of these weapons increased the hazards the troops faced. As Doughboy Elton Mackin wrote, "What do men think about at such a time? . . . [I]s my number up today?"

> "The mushy fields bubbled like a bowl of porridge as big shells, little shells, and medium-sized shells kissed the mud."
>
> —Charles MacArthur, 1918

CHAPTER SEVEN

DOUGHBOY HEROES MEET THE BOCHE

"Every soldier at the moment of battle trembles, is afraid and wishes he could escape from it," wrote Doughboy Will Judy. "[E]ach one is watchful lest a companion may read fear in his face. . . . [T]he whole regiment goes into battle, playing the part of bravery, yet sick of the whole business." As the Doughboys engaged in battle, they knew they would be tested. It was a test all the Allies were hoping they would pass.

The Doughboys in the American Expeditionary Force had been placed in sections of the trenches that had not been under German attack for some time. These sections were considered safer.

The Allied command-
ers determined that
this was the best way
for the Doughboys to
become used to the
fighting. From the
beginning, however,
the plan to place

"Every soldier at the moment of battle trembles, is afraid and wishes he could escape from it."

–Will Judy, 1930, in reference to his experience in 1918

them in the so-called quiet parts of the line went wrong. Sure
enough, these sections suddenly stopped being quiet.

STIRRING THINGS UP

There were two theories why this happened. The first was that the
Germans were trying to test the new troops. Whenever they were
facing Americans, the Germans would be given orders to "go over
the top"—come out of their trenches and launch an attack. They
wanted to see how the Americans responded.

The other theory was that the Americans had a different
approach than the rest of the Allies. The French and the British were
in the trenches day after day without initiating much fighting. The
Americans, on the other hand, were always stirring things up.
Soldier H. W. Ross tells a story he heard from an American in the
trenches. The American was warned by the French not to start trouble by shooting at the Germans. The U.S. soldier replied, "That's what
we're here for."

Whatever the cause of the increased activity by the German
troops along the line, the Americans responded well to their first
taste of battle. They fought off attacks as they came. They generally
caused exactly the trouble that Ross said the French wanted to avoid.
"Yes, The Kaiser's [Germany's ruler] Sure We're On The Western Front

Now," said the headline in *Stars and Stripes* on March 8, 1918. The article continued, "The Americans came out of the biggest attack yet with infinite credit."

Of course, causing trouble gave the Doughboys a bitter taste of the war that was still to come. "Our trenches were about 800 yards from the German trenches," wrote Doughboy Clyde Grimsley of a surprise attack at dawn by the German soldiers. "A grenade struck the parapet [wall] in front of us and my buddies and I were hit . . . we were helpless."

The Americans arrived at a time when German spirits were low. German officer Rudolf Binding

German troops pass the time in the trenches early in the war *(below)*. By the time the Americans arrived, many German troops were already physically and mentally exhausted.

> "The physical exhaustion of the infantry . . . was so great . . . they let themselves be slowly wiped out by the enemy's artillery fire almost without caring."
>
> —Rudolf Binding, 1918

described the state of the soldiers in his diary entry of April 22, 1918, "The physical exhaustion of the infantry . . . was so great . . . they let themselves be slowly wiped out by the enemy's artillery fire almost without caring." With the Germans worn out, the fresh U.S. troops played a major role in turning the tide of the war.

WORTHY OPPONENTS

At the same time, another factor made the German commanders take action. Germany had been fighting a war on two fronts: on the western front against the French and the British and on the eastern front against Russia. Due to losses on the battlefield, the Russians had been forced to ditch the Allies and plead for peace with the Germans. This freed up thousands of skilled, successful German troops to go to the western front and support the discouraged troops. They were Germany's last best chance to break the western front.

The Germans had to act before U.S. troops could be fully mobilized. The Germans chose to attack. On May 27, 1918, they began an advance that would take them within 60 miles of Paris. At first it seemed that the Germans were unstoppable. They quickly rolled through the French and British troops in their path.

U.S. troops were rushed into position. The U.S. and German armies met near Château-Thierry and nearby at Belleau Wood.

The series of attacks lasted for most of June. It was the Doughboys' first major engagement. The twenty-eight thousand untested Americans were told they would be fighting Germany's best soldiers, who would outnumber them five to one. One group of eight thousand U.S. Marines fighting in the battle suffered more than five thousand casualties. A soldier in the unit, Carl Brannen, remembered the effect of the shells on the human body. They caused the victim to "rain down in pieces."

Yet, despite their losses, the Americans were determined fighters. The Germans quickly learned to fear their new enemy. At one point, the Doughboys captured a section of the woods six separate times. At another they resorted to bayonets and hand-to-hand combat. In spite of casualties, the Americans just kept coming back until the job was done and they had taken the ground. A German report on the fighting at Belleau Wood reported, "The nerves of the Americans are still unshaken." The report detailed the Doughboys' "careless confidence" and said they were "a very worthy opponent."

> ## "The nerves of the Americans are still unshaken."
> —German report, 1918

Private Walter Spearing was one of the eighteen hundred Americans who died in the fighting at Belleau Wood. His best friend, Private Segal, kept the promise they had made to each other. If one of them died, the other would write to console the victim's mother. "Walt is well avenged . . . he has not died in vain," the letter reads, and "his spirit leads us on to ultimate victory." The number of American dead and wounded was nearly ten thousand.

Even the Germans were shocked at how "terribly reckless" the Americans were in battle. Private Herbert K. Lennox was a good example of the fierceness of the American fighters. He described an attack when he wrote home to his parents in June. He was wounded "when the Huns put a barrage on our line." Determined to get back at the enemy, he pulled himself to his feet and grabbed an automatic rifle. Then, seeing that he was facing the enemy only 20 feet away, "I started on one end of their line and began mowing them down," until he was wounded again.

This painting from 1944 depicts the brutal fighting that took place at Belleau Wood in France.

The American Expeditionary Force stopped the German advance. It was the beginning of the end for the Germans. Lieutenant Quincy Mills, writing to his mother in July 1918, captured the reality of what the U.S. victories had already achieved. "The backbone of Prussian [German] aggression has been broken," he wrote. No one need fear any longer that "a vast tidal wave of barbarism" would destroy the world.

From July 1918 on, there would be one hard-fought battle after another as the Germans were steadily driven back into Germany. Doughboy John Clark celebrated his birthday on July 19 on the battle-field as part of a surprise attack on German lines. "It is now open war-fare," he wrote in his diary. "Movement carried on irrespective of whether it is day or night. . . . I am just beginning to realize what war is."

ATTACK AT SAINT–MIHIEL

For the Americans, some of their greatest glory would occur in the fighting that began on September 12, 1918. The army, finally under its own command, began forcing the Germans from the Saint–Mihiel salient. The salient was an area where the line of battle jutted 40 miles into France. The French had not been able to drive off the German troops. The salient had to be cleared before the next phase of the offensive could begin.

The fighting was fierce. Charles MacArthur was serving in an artillery unit of the famed Rainbow Division, one of the bravest and mostly highly decorated military units in the AEF. He described the scene as the Americans attacked at Saint–Mihiel: "A murderous salvo . . . there were so many explosions that our target was obscured by the smoke." Then "the Germans got real rough, slinging iron like confetti."

These first few days of the battle were intense. The Americans took on a task that the French army had twice attempted and failed.

Three brave Doughboys go over the top at the charge of the Saint–Mihiel salient. The victory at Saint–Mihiel recaptured an important piece of land for the Allies.

The Doughboys managed to force the Germans from territory that the Germans had held for the entire four years of the war. A week later, the difficult and danger-ous job was done. Both the Allies and the Germans were shocked by the Doughboys' quick success. But it was only a sign of the fighting to come.

THE AIR WAR

At the same time that the war was being fought on the ground, a war was also taking place in the air. Planes had been used throughout the war. But they were less effective than the commanders had hoped. At the end of the war, the planes were becoming much more useful.

TRAINING FOR YET MORE WAR

World War I and World War II were only twenty-one years apart. The generation that fought as Doughboys in World War I became the military leaders of World War II. Two of the great generals of World War II met for the first time on the Saint-Mihiel battlefield where they both served.

Douglas MacArthur was a graduate of West Point Military Academy and a brigadier general in the AEF in 1918. He already had fifteen years of military service. George S. Patton was also a West Point graduate, but he was only a lieutenant colonel with a mere nine years of military experience. The men had never met each other until Saint-Mihiel brought them together on a fateful day.

It was September 12, and MacArthur was in charge of an attack on German lines by the 84th Brigade. Patton was trying to find out why some of the tanks under his command had gotten stuck. The two men met each other just as the enemy began to attack. As everyone headed for cover, the two men supposedly stood calmly talking with each other. Neither of them were willing to let the other think they were frightened by the shells falling all around them. Patton wrote to his wife about the incident a few days later. MacArthur talked about it in his memoirs, which were written almost fifty years after the event.

Douglas MacArthur went on to be the hero of the Philippines in World War II. He was on the deck of the USS *Missouri* to accept the surrender of the Japanese on September 2, 1945. George S. Patton became the legendary tank commander whose actions in Africa, Sicily, and the final attack on Germany helped defeat Hitler in World War II.

The planes were primitive, made of wood and canvas. They flew at less than 100 miles per hour and were used for a very limited range. French pilot Jean Villars wrote about feeling vulnerable while flying in battle. He wrote of being "in the midst of innumerable passing shells. . . . [E]ach detonation shakes us in our seats."

American George Hughes wrote home to his mother with a

similar feeling. "It's only one in about forty thousand shells that brings a ship down," he told her, "but when a pilot begins to hear those old high explosives breaking around him ... he [is] feeling that the forty thousandth shell may be about to arrive with his full name and address written on its side."

> "... in the midst of innumerable passing shells.... [E]ach detonation shakes us in our seats."
>
> —Jean Villars, 1916

It was this sense of danger that perhaps made the planes so romantic and glorious. The pilots who flew them, especially those who became aces—the superstars of air combat—earned great glory. U.S. captain Eddie

Rickenbacker was the United States' top ace. He was responsible for downing twenty-six enemy planes, or kills. Famed German pilot Manfred von Richthofen was nicknamed the Red Baron. He beat out all the pilots in the war with eighty kills.

U.S. captain Eddie Rickenbacker stands next to his plane in a field near Toul, France, in 1918. Rickenbacker was a race car driver before joining the war effort and becoming a pilot.

German flying ace Manfred von Richthofen was called the Red Baron because he painted his Fokker triplane bright red.

For the Doughboy on the ground, the air wars were of little interest. That is, until Colonel William Mitchell decided to try to use the planes in the U.S. attack on the Saint–Mihiel salient. For the first time, there was coordination between an air attack and a ground assault. It happened late in the war, but it gave a picture of how important airpower could be.

BEHIND THE SCENES

Coordinating a war in the air and on the ground became more and more complex. The need for better communication and management was obvious. Major General William Wright was in charge of the 89th Division from the battle at Saint–Mihiel to the end of the war. He wrote in his memoir about the duties behind the scenes.

General Wright went everywhere, observing the conditions at the hospitals and visiting the troops when they were brought back from the lines. He noted their conditions and their morale. "Stopped and talked to the men. Saw them getting their supper; getting clean clothes; were in good spirits," he recorded in his diary on September 23, 1918.

Every once in a while, the pain of what he was seeing filtered in. This happened on the day he saw the bodies of two U.S. troops who had lain unburied for several days. He ordered their immediate burial and removed their identification tags himself.

THE MEUSE-ARGONNE OFFENSIVE

The Doughboys began the final offensive of World War I on September 26, 1918. Their attack would take place in the dense woods of the Argonne Forest. Charles MacArthur joked at the beginning of the campaign, "The mushy fields bubbled like a bowl of porridge as big shells, little shells, and medium-sized shells kissed the mud.... We could see right off that the Argonne wasn't going to be any fun at all." Immediately the troops "flattened out.... It wasn't safe to wiggle your ears."

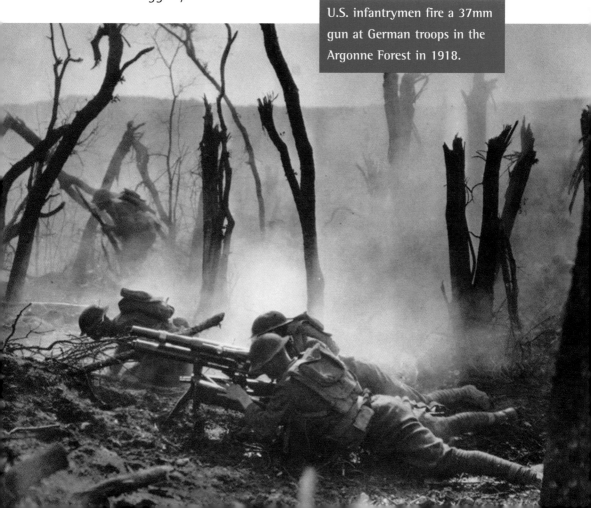

U.S. infantrymen fire a 37mm gun at German troops in the Argonne Forest in 1918.

William Langer was also part of the attack. He remembered "the shells literally rained about." He admitted that he had not "expected to get away alive." Many did not. More than twenty-six thousand Americans died in the Meuse-Argonne offensive.

Louis Ranlett was one of the lucky ones who would recover from his wounds. His unit had joined the campaign on October 3. He dictated in a letter home, "After four days' dodging I failed to hear a high-explosive and allowed it to land in front of me with the result that a small piece got into my left eye." He would never see with that eye again, but for him the war was over. He returned home.

Lieutenant Harry Spring had the chance to see more of the results of the fighting than most of the troops during the battle. He was an engineer in a unit that supported three regiments. They helped with bridges, power plants, and other engineering needs. In his diary, Spring described getting a power plant working in the middle of heavy enemy shelling. Sent to another location a few days later, he recorded "Quite a number of dead Boche along the way as well as dead Doughboys and horses. Snipers active all over. Certainly a horrible sight."

In the end, the Meuse-Argonne offensive drove Kaiser Wilhelm, the German leader, to step down. Two days later, on November 11, 1918, the Germans surrendered.

On all levels, the Doughboys proved that they could more than handle themselves in battle.

> "Quite a number of dead Boche along the way as well as dead Doughboys and horses. Snipers active all over. Certainly a horrible sight."
>
> –Harry Spring, 1918

VISITING WORLD WAR I SITES

The western front of World War I became a battleground again in 1939. Many of the areas where the Doughboys fought—the trenches and fortifications—were reused by the Allies in World War II. Not many battlegrounds are associated only with the Doughboys. However, there are several places where their presence can be found.

The best of these sites is the battlefield at Belleau Wood and its companion monument to U.S. troops at Château-Thierry, France. Visitors can also travel to Verdun. They can walk through well-preserved bunkers at places such as Fort Vaux to get a feel for life along the battle lines. And the Ossuary at Douaumont, France, gives visitors a sense of how many lives were lost.

There are also sites where grateful Europeans have erected monuments to the Doughboys so they will never be forgotten. These include the Monfaucon and Montsec (Thiaucourt) American monuments on the Saint–Mihiel salient. The graves of the Doughboys who never came home from the war show the American sacrifice even more clearly. Visitors can see the Aisne-Marne American Cemetery at Belleau Wood or the cemeteries at Saint–Mihiel and the Meuse-Argonne.

They were heroes, honored by their allies for their bravery and respected by their enemies for their strength. In the witty words of Charles MacArthur, regarding one of the fights in the Argonne Forest, "It was a great day for the doughboys . . . spent a hot hour stabbing, and getting stabbed, and winning washtubs full of crosses and Medals of Honor."

> **"I didn't even want to take a dead mouse out of a trap when I was home."**
>
> —Robert Hoffman, 1940, commenting on life after the war

CHAPTER EIGHT

AFTER THE BATTLES

When the battles ended, for many, the horrors were just beginning. "While picking up a man who had been hit dead center above the eyes ... the dead man's brains slopped messily over Slim's shoes," wrote Elton Mackin of his first day on burial duty at Belleau Wood.

German Rudolf Binding spoke of the "peculiar sour, heavy, and penetrating smell of corpses." He also discussed seeing a British soldier's corpse still in the front of a trench. He noted that "a little brook runs through the trench, and everyone uses the water for drinking and washing.... Nobody minds the pale Englishman who is rotting away a few steps farther up."

U.S. engineer Harry Spring was on burial duty. He found "one poor American lad was clutching a picture of a girl in his hand." German officer Ernst Jünger wrote of the horror of "the dead ... left month after month to the mercy of wind and weather."

These U.S. casualties are half-buried in a shallow grave outside of the Argonne Forest in 1918.

Robert Hoffman recalled being in charge of removing the personal effects from the bodies of seventy-eight American Doughboys one morning. "It was not pleasant," he wrote, "but I managed to eat my quota of bread and meat when it came up with no opportunity to wash my hands." He noted his family's concern that his experiences with death would make him "hard, brutal, callous." Instead, he explained, "I didn't even want to take a dead mouse out of a trap when I was home."

THE HOSPITALS

Sometimes even civilian Americans found themselves closer to the horror of battle than they intended to be. When the United States entered the war, Guy Bowerman Jr. was a student at Yale University and too young to qualify for the draft. Instead, he joined the U.S. Ambulance Service. He found himself closer to the front lines than he expected. "This dressing station to which the men are brought," he wrote, "is about an [eighth] of a mile from the front line. Shells were whistling over head and on both sides."

For the wounded after a battle, the prospect of going home weighed against concerns about what would happen to them on the way there. Lieutenant Ralph Robart was relieved to arrive at the hospital. "Life seemed kind regardless of our wounds," he remembered. "We were happy with the let down, with clean beds and three meals a day. It was like going from Hell to Heaven."

The hospital was a haven for all the wounded. It was the one place where they knew they would receive treatment whether they

STATISTICS ON U.S. PARTICIPATION IN WORLD WAR I

Population of the United States: 102,800,000

Number of U.S. troops: 4,743,800

Percent of participation: 4.6 percent

American deaths in combat: 53,513

Other troop deaths (disease, accident, etc.): 63,195

Wounded: 204,002

Death rate: 2.7 percent

Overall casualty rate: 6.8 percent

Source: U.S. Department of Defense

were friend or foe. British nurse Vera Brittain found herself caring for wounded German prisoners. "The majority are more or less dying," she wrote to her mother. "One forgets that they are the enemy and can only remember that they are suffering beings."

Some of the troops spent a lot of time in the hospital but without injuries that would give them their ticket home. Private Frank Moyer of the Rainbow Division was one such soldier. Writing home in 1918, he was on his third stay at the hospital. His first was for a minor shrapnel wound. His second was for trench foot and boils. The third time, he was the victim of a mustard gas attack. He had been blinded at first but was grateful that "now I can see again."

PRISONERS

There was one fear shared by French and British troops that most of the American Doughboys did not suffer: being taken prisoner by the enemy. Early in the war, many of the Allied troops were taken

WOUNDS THAT DON'T SHOW

When U.S. armies go off to battle, their commanders are concerned with their physical health. This has always been the case. Generals need healthy soldiers to fight the wars. In modern times, generals have also become concerned with soldiers' mental health. Medical texts have shown that many soldiers come home scarred for life, even when they don't receive physical wounds. This is known as posttraumatic stress disorder.

Accounts from long before the Great War tell of soldiers who ran from the fighting, froze, and were unable to fight or acted strangely after battle. However, these were seen as unusual and fleeting episodes. Soldiers in the Civil War, for example, might face the intensity of a three-day battle at someplace such as Gettysburg. Most battles ended within days, and there were long time periods in which the soldiers faced only boredom. In World War I, the soldiers remained under battle conditions in the trenches for months at a time. There was no opportunity for escape. As a result, World War I is the first war that began to emphasize the mental health of the soldiers.

The science of psychiatry also changed. Psychiatrists began to study and measure the numbers of veterans who suffered mental trauma from their wartime experiences. Doctors began to speak of shell shock. This described soldiers who developed mental problems after long periods of time under battle conditions. Once psychiatry became part of war, generals had to consider the mental state of their soldiers when choosing strategies and tactics.

prisoner after battles. Soon after their arrival in France, a few Americans did fall prisoner to the Germans. An article in *Stars and Stripes* described their treatment: "Ridicule, degrading labor, insufficient food and inhumane treatment generally are the lot of American troops taken prisoner by the Hun." Fortunately, it was not a common occurrence for the Doughboys. Since they quickly went on the offensive in the war, the Doughboys were taking prisoners instead of becoming prisoners.

As the war ended and all prisoners were released, the German government issued a pamphlet defending their treatment of prisoners of war. It was intended for British prisoners, but the message referred to the treatment of all prisoners taken during the war. "There were many discomforts, irritations, misunderstandings. Your situation has been a difficult one," said the pamphlet. "We know that errors have been committed and that there have been hardships."

This was a curious admission to be sending home with the freed prisoners. Perhaps the German government thought this message would make up for the experiences Allied prisoners had suffered as captives.

> "Ridicule, degrading labor, insufficient food and inhumane treatment generally are the lot of American troops taken prisoner by the Hun."
>
> –*Stars and Stripes*, 1918

> **"If I made mistakes, some would die on their stretchers on the floor... who need not have died."**
> —Mary Borden, 1929, in reference to her experience during World War I

CHAPTER NINE

AMERICAN WOMEN AT WORK

Less than one hundred years ago, women couldn't have any supporting role in wartime. During the Civil War, fewomen had any sort of recognized official work World War I, on the other hand, gave women the chance to perform tasks that had previously been handled only by men.

At home in the United States, more than 3 million women moved into industries to replace the male workers who had gone off to fight. They worked in factories, making everything from clothing to tanks and weapons. They worked the farms. They helped build ships. For women frustrated by the rules of society, this was a chance to show the world what women could do.

An estimated twenty-five thousand American women went overseas. Many of them went because it gave them a chance to do things that society would never have allowed. One woman noted: "Within that tightly structured existence, women on the Western Front found a new sense of freedom, a personal freedom . . . that was exhilarating . . . a freedom to make basic decisions for one's way of life."

Women who served still performed jobs that were traditionally considered women's work. They served as secretaries, hostesses, telephone operators, and nurses. Although the women did not fight in the war, they did make similar sacrifices and suffer similar hardships. More than three hundred of them died. Some fell prey to disease. Others, serving close to enemy lines, were killed by shellfire.

YEOMANETTES

The amount of paperwork involved in running the American Expeditionary Force was huge. This gave women an opportunity to travel overseas as secretaries and

Enlisted navy women stand on the White House lawn in 1918. From 1918 to 1925, women were allowed to enlist in the U.S. Navy. In 1942 a law was passed that again allowed women to enlist so they could serve in World War II.

stenographers. Enrolled as Yeoman (F), for female, they rapidly gained the nickname Yeomanettes to distinguish them from their male colleagues.

Helen Dunbar McCrery became one of the Yeomanettes performing secretarial tasks in the U.S. Navy. "They needed girls who had stenographic skills," she wrote. "I was good at it." These women did not have easy jobs. They worked long hours, often working sixty hours a week at their duties.

The navy had its Yeomanettes in place by the time the United States entered the war. As other branches of the military saw how useful they were, women gained more opportunities to serve. The U.S. Marines resisted the idea of women working among them until August 1918. Then they began recruiting women with the slogan, "Free a Man to Fight."

Estimates of the number of women involved in war-related work overseas vary widely. However, at least eleven thousand women yeomen were doing secretarial work for the military. Records show that at least twenty-two of the Yeomanettes died overseas.

DOUGHNUT GIRLS AND HELLO GIRLS

Both the Salvation Army and the American Red Cross ran canteens for the Doughboys. The women who worked there were often known as doughnut girls. This was because many of the canteens offered the troops coffee and doughnuts. The women lived in groups at decent homes and were closely chaperoned.

Red Cross workers had additional duties. They helped wounded troops contact family members. They also collected information about dead soldiers to be sent to the families back home.

The Hello Girls filled a military need of the U.S. Army Signal Corps. The army needed the male members of the signal corps to

PARLEZ-VOUS ANGLAIS?

World War I brought the advent of a wonderful new technology, the telephone. With it came a new method for the general staff's management of the battlefield. However, the commanders of the American Expeditionary Force encountered an unexpected problem. Communication would have to go through telephone operators, and the fighting was taking place in a country where the citizens did not speak English. U.S. military officers were not fluent in French.

Communications were supposed to be handled by the U.S. Army Signal Corps. The men in the corps were too busy trying to keep telephone lines in place and in working order to learn a new language. The signal corps members did not have enough people to solve the language problem.

The solution was ingenious. It was also controversial in a society where women were considered too delicate to be exposed to war. The U.S. military asked the Bell Telephone Company to recruit telephone operators who could speak both English and French. They also had to be willing to become members of the signal corps for the entire war. Thus were born the Hello Girls and with them the idea that women could be of strategic value in waging war.

string and maintain telephone lines. A limited number of workers were available. The Bell Telephone Company recruited women to become members of the signal corps. They were actually sworn into the army as soldiers. These women worked long hours on the switchboard to keep communications open for military use.

Hello Girls needed to speak two languages because they worked in France. They were constantly talking to French telephone operators. A group of them received citations for bravery. They remained at their switchboards during a critical part of the battle at Saint-Mihiel, even after the building they were working in caught fire.

Nurses

Nursing had perhaps the greatest personal impact on the lives of the Doughboys. It was a demanding and frustrating profession for women. They were helping wounded men get healthy enough to be sent back to the trenches.

There was a severe shortage of nurses during the war. Those who were available worked long, hard hours in the hospitals. Because of this, historian Susan Grayzel commented that "the women found themselves performing previously unthinkable tasks."

Nurse Mary Borden had the job of sorting the wounded as they arrived. She decided the order in which the soldiers would receive treatment. She

American nurses wearing protective clothing walk through a trench in France in 1918.

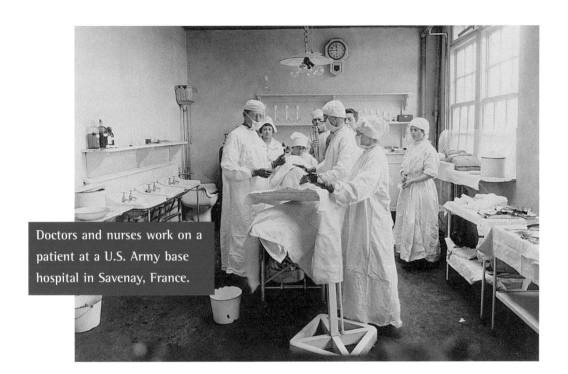

Doctors and nurses work on a patient at a U.S. Army base hospital in Savenay, France.

remembered: "If I made mistakes, some would die on their stretchers on the floor... who need not have died. I didn't worry. I didn't think. I was too busy, too absorbed in what I was doing."

Women's tasks abroad did not end when the fighting stopped. Margaret Lambie served in a U.S. relief unit. It was responsible for aiding refugees returning home as the war ended. It also helped families seeking to find their dead loved ones. It was unpleasant duty at best. "People come from all parts of France to locate graves of lost husbands, sons and brothers. . . . One mother discovered her twenty-year old son only half buried. Many find no trace." In a nation that would bury 130,000 unknown soldiers, there were many people to be assisted and consoled.

Another important task came to American women as the war ended. More than two thousand women answered the call after it was discovered that the troops "recovered more rapidly when occupied."

This job is known in modern times as occupational therapy. These therapists help the wounded recover their ability to perform everyday tasks. They also help them adjust to the new realities of their lives.

This was not a job that could be done only by nurses. Some of these women were former teachers, artists, secretaries, and more. Mary Wrinn was one of the women involved in this important work. She discussed the need to help these wounded: "The same impulse that had sent the soldier to face death, now sent her to help him live again."

There was a strong feeling among women that this war provided them with an opportunity to expand the horizons for all women. However, all the changes that

Women also took factory jobs during the war to replace the men who were overseas. The women in this photo, taken in 1918, are chipping wooden blocks with pneumatic hammers. Once the war was over, they were expected to leave their jobs.

occurred for women during wartime did not bring about permanent change in the workplace. As one historian notes, "Similar to other nations, American women's advances into previously masculine industrial workplace and occupations did not extend long past the war." Another historian noted, "The war had proved to be a hoax for women's hopes of liberation."

> "The same impulse that had sent the soldier to face death, now sent her to help him live again."
>
> –Mary Wrinn, in reference to her experience in 1918

CHAPTER TEN

WINNERS AND LOSERS

"The Germans meant to win," wrote American reporter Frederick Palmer. "I always thought of them as having the spirit of the Middle Ages in their hearts, organized for victory by every modern method." But the Germans lost, and it was an embarrassing defeat, in part because it was to the inexperienced Americans.

John Clark was surprised at how welcome the Allies felt as they arrived in Germany. "They are most cordial and pleasant," he wrote. "[T]hey look upon us more as deliverers and forerunners of a better day, than as conquerors."

Even the German soldiers seemed ready to accept their defeat in the early days after the end of the war. Rudolf Binding wrote on the day of the truce, "I must say that I can watch this disintegration of the Army almost without feeling upset. I had already gone through it all in [my] mind. When it happened I hardly felt it."

The disagreements in the United States about the war did not fade away with the great Allied victory. Many Americans of German descent stayed angry. They were angry first that the United States had joined the war and second that the Germans had been defeated by the U.S. military.

Minne Allen was a German citizen married to an American professor. She always believed that her fatherland would be able to resist the Americans. Her letters to her mother in Germany speak of American "arrogance" and "thickheadedness" and "egotism." Allen's husband shared her somewhat extreme views. He wrote to his mother-in-law after the war was over of the "victory of arrogance and hate that we couldn't then have imagined."

THE ARMISTICE

The armistice (truce) was signed on November 11, 1918. General William Wright ordered the fighting to "stop exactly at eleven o'clock and the

U.S. president Woodrow Wilson reads the armistice terms to Congress on November 11, 1918.

men would dig in on the ground they occupied." He also ordered that there not "be any hilarity or demonstration on the part of my troops." A quiet end came to what one soldier had described as "a terrible travesty of civilization . . . ridiculous . . . just like two boys getting madder and madder until they are fairly consuming themselves in a perfect frenzy of hate."

For the Doughboys themselves, the "magic" moment occurred at exactly eleven o'clock that morning. It was the moment when each of them knew that he was going home. "On the stroke of 11 the cannon stopped, the rifles dropped from the shoulders, the machine guns grew still. There followed a strange, unbelievable silence as though the world had died," according to the article in *Stars and Stripes.*

The joy that followed turned into frustration as the troops waited to be sent home. It had taken a year to get all the Doughboys to France. There was no way they could now all go home at once. Troops' accounts speak of "gloom" as they impatiently waited their turn to board the boats to go home. About 250,000 troops went home each month, but to those still waiting, the time seemed endless.

> "On the stroke of 11 the cannon stopped, the rifles dropped from the shoulders, the machine guns grew still. There followed a strange, unbelievable silence as though the world had died."
>
> —*Stars and Stripes,* 1918

Even after their unit was chosen to go home, they had to deal with hassles and delays. A routine delousing took place before departure. The army command didn't want the troops to carry home lice.

Doughboys, frustrated and exhausted, wait to depart France and start their long journey back to the United States.

For the troops, being sent through "the mill," as the delousing procedure was called, meant they were leaving soon, before they could become reinfected with the pests.

Crowded onto ships that were filled well beyond their normal capacity, the Doughboys endured the trip home. Arrival was sweet indeed. One Texas unit was greeted at Newport News, Virginia, as they arrived with "the sounds of music from several bands" and food and "other little delicacies befitting the occasion." From their arrival ports, they dealt with another round of delousing. Then the Doughboys boarded trains. The trains took them to the military camps closest to their homes for discharge from the army.

HOME AT LAST

At home the troops were greeted with parades and excitement. Although bringing home German helmets, guns, and other gear was not allowed, the rule was rarely enforced. With these souvenirs from battle, they returned to civilian life.

The soldiers were pretty much forgotten by the government and the army that had needed their services so desperately the year before. One website sums up their veterans' benefits as "a suit of civilian clothes, a pair of medals, and a small cash payment." It also notes that those who did not go off to war ended up "a lot better off than those who had."

Coming home was a difficult adjustment. Their experiences influenced them to fight for the rights of those U.S. troops who

U.S. soldiers who fought overseas in World War I march past the New York Public Library in a huge victory parade in 1918.

fought in the next great war. Making sure that all troops were well treated became one last battle for the Doughboys.

In 1944 the next generation of soldiers was off fighting in World War II. Meanwhile, the veteran Doughboys passed the Servicemen's Readjustment Act, called the GI Bill. The next troops that came home from war found that "wartime military service became a steppingstone to a better life."

In its own way, the GI Bill was one of the greatest services these citizen-soldier Doughboys ever gave to their country. They learned many lessons from preparing for battle. Later, they made sure the government learned these lessons as well. This led the U.S. armed forces to become the best in the world.

THE AFTERMATH

World War I is one of the most difficult wars to sum up. In so many ways, it was a war of great expectations, but it resolved little. In fact, the bitter peace settlement that finally ended this "war to end all wars" sowed the seeds for a wider and even more destructive war—World War II. In Germany the harsh peace terms hurt the economy. Germans fumed at their fate. The unrest that followed led to the rise of Adolf Hitler.

In the United States, the hoped-for social change among those who had found new jobs during the war never took place. Women had made great strides during the war by working in jobs traditionally closed to them. But after the war, they quietly slipped back into society.

African American men and women had served overseas as soldiers and other support staff. Yet, they came home to the same old restrictions that had been in place before the war. One African American woman had worked as a secretary for the YMCA in Paris.

THE FORGOTTEN WAR

World War I has been called the Great War and the "war to end all wars." But it's also the most forgotten of modern U.S. wars. The U.S. monuments built for the Doughboys are neither as elaborate nor as numerous as those honoring troops of other conflicts.

The American Expeditionary Force Monument in Washington, D.C., is the official national monument of World War I. The monument is located on Pennsylvania Avenue. It is smaller and less striking than the monuments dedicated to the troops of World War II, the Korean War (1950–1953), and the Vietnam War (1957–1975).

The monument is a statue of General John J. Pershing, commander of the American Expeditionary Force. It shows an excerpt from his tribute to his troops and their courage in Europe. It reads in part, "The American Expeditionary Forces have left a heritage of whom those who follow may ever be proud." The troops were honored with a federal holiday celebrating their victory. Called Armistice Day, the holiday later became a celebration of all veterans and is now called Veterans' Day.

In small towns and big cities across the country, plaques and statues honor the service of the Doughboys. Monuments in France show gratitude for U.S. participation in the war, including an impressive one at Château–Thierry *(below)*. However, World War II followed very soon after the Great War. And the Doughboys returned home to a country taken over by the flu and then thrown into an economic depression. Because of this, World War I did not excite people the way the memories of the Civil War did. The marvelous accomplishments of the Doughboys seemed to be lost in the flood of history that followed their return home.

Members of the all-African American 369th Infantry Regiment celebrate the Allied victory as they arrive in New York City in 1919.

She found that white secretaries had "brought their native prejudice with them" to France. She was told on the ship home that "colored people need not expect any such treatment as had been given them by the French."

President Woodrow Wilson's dreams of a new world order through the international League of Nations also did not come to pass. President Wilson had hoped to create a group of nations that would work together to avoid wars in the future. In the end, Congress voted against joining the League of Nations, and the world was unable to avoid another war.

An unexpected change did occur. The United States became a major power in the world. U.S. leadership had defied the Allied plans to use the U.S. military "as a replacement depot" for "their depleted ranks." The U.S. command proved that the United States, although unprepared for war, could quickly mobilize its military into a strong fighting force.

The United States might have had a small standing army. It might have stumbled along while trying to build up its military and get it into the fight. But once they began fighting, the Doughboys showed that U.S. soldiers and sailors were a great force. From these first steps in World War I, the United States moved steadily forward as a leader in world politics.

The people of Great Britain and France would remember their American allies' role in the victory. French soldier René Arnaud spoke in his memoirs of his first meeting with the Doughboys. They "boosted my hope and confidence. . . . I have never forgotten this brief moment of exaltation, and I have always retained a deep sense of gratitude for those who helped us in our moment of need and turned the scales in our favour."

> They "boosted my hope and confidence. . . . I have never forgotten this brief moment of exaltation, and I have always retained a deep sense of gratitude for those who helped us in our moment of need and turned the scales in our favour."
>
> –René Arnaudené Arnaud, 1918

Those Doughboys had indeed fully repaid the debt to France for its help in the Revolutionary War. The great powers of Europe would soon realize that they had awakened an awesome presence. This presence would impact the course of human history throughout the coming century and into the next millennium.

The Doughboys returned home proud of what they had accomplished. The adventure that they had sought stayed with them for the rest of their lives. William Upson said it best for all of them. "Good old Army! Good old War! It's given us something to talk about and think about for all the rest of [our] lives. I wouldn't have missed it for ten thousand dollars, but I wouldn't re-enlist for ten million."

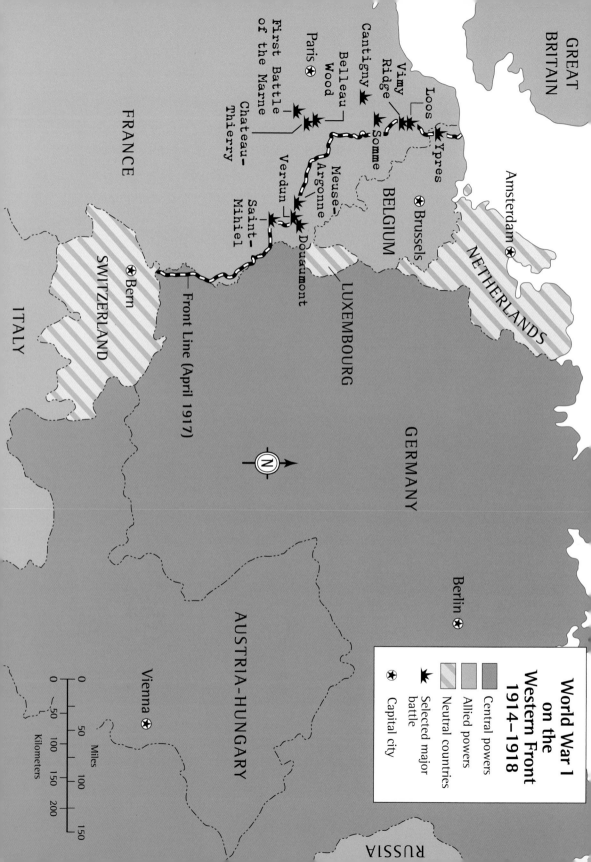

World War 1
on the
Western Front
1914–1918

Neutral countries
Allied powers
Central powers

Selected major
battle

Capital city

GREAT BRITAIN

FRANCE

PARIS

First Battle
of the Marne

Chateau-
Thierry

Belleau
Wood

Cantigny

Vimy
Ridge

Loos

Ypres

Somme

Meuse-
Argonne

Verdun

Saint-
Mihiel

Douaumont

BELGIUM

Brussels

LUXEMBOURG

NETHERLANDS

Amsterdam

SWITZERLAND

Bern

Front Line (April 1917)

ITALY

GERMANY

Berlin

AUSTRIA-HUNGARY

Vienna

RUSSIA

N

0   50   100 150
Miles

0   50 100 150 200
Kilometers

Chronology of World War I

August 4, 1914	Germany invades neutral Belgium in a surprise attack that causes Allied nations Great Britain and France to declare war on Germany.
September 5–10, 1914	The first Battle of the Marne halts the German invasion.
September 15, 1914	Both sides begin entrenching along the line that becomes known as the western front.
May 7, 1915	A German U-boat sinks the *Lusitania*, killing 1,198 civilians, including 128 Americans.
August 30, 1915	Germany agrees to the U.S. demand to stop attacking neutral ships.
July 1–November 18, 1916	The Battle of the Somme results in more than 1 million casualties, but the war is still a stalemate.
November 7, 1916	Woodrow Wilson is reelected president using the slogan, "He kept us out of war."
February 1, 1917	Germany announces its resumption of unrestricted submarine warfare.
April 6, 1917	President Wilson asks Congress for a declaration of war against Germany.
July 3, 1917	The first Doughboys reach France.
October 23, 1917	The first Doughboys are assigned to trenches.
March 21, 1918	German forces begin a series of offensives to break through the lines before the U.S. military can reinforce it.
May 28, 1918	U.S. troops win their first major engagement at the battle at Cantigny.
May 31, 1918	German advance stopped by U.S. troops at Château-Thierry.

June 6, 1918	Doughboys are successful at Belleau Wood.
September 12, 1918	Doughboys drive German forces from Saint-Mihiel.
September 26, 1918	The Meuse-Argonne offensive begins.
November 11, 1918	At the eleventh hour on the eleventh day of the eleventh month, the Germans and the Allies sign an armistice, effectively ending the war.
June 28, 1919	A peace treaty ending the war is signed at Versailles, France.

Source Notes

10 I. L. Read, *Of Those We Loved* (Edinburgh, UK: Pentland Press, 1994), 259.

13 Christian Mallett, *Impressions and Experiences of a French Trooper 1914–1915* (London: Constable & Company, 1916), 133.

13 Donald C. Richter, ed., *Lionel Sotheby's Great War* (Athens: Ohio University Press, 1997), 113.

13 Ibid., 133.

13 Ibid., 138.

14 Sydney Giffard, *Guns, Kites and Horses* (London: Radcliffe Press, 2003), 51.

14 Alan Bishop and Mark Bostridge, ed., *Letters from a Lost Generation* (Boston: Northeastern University Press, 1998), 113.

14 Read, 259.

15 Malcolm Brown, *The Imperial War Museum Book of the First World War* (Norman: University of Oklahoma Press, 1993), 50.

15 Ibid., 55.

16 George Connes, *A POW's Memoir of the First World War* (Oxford, UK: Berg, 2004), 13.

16 Antoine Redier, *Comrades in Courage* (Garden City, NY: Doubleday, Page & Company, 1918), 33, 40.

17 Lyn MacDonald, *The Roses of No Man's Land* (London: Michael Joseph, 1980), 139.

17 Edwin Austin Abbey, *An American Soldier* (Boston: Houghton Mifflin Company, 1918), 13–14.

18 Ibid., 165.

18 Frederick Libby, *Horses Don't Fly* (New York: Arcade Publishing, 2000), 117.

19 Ibid., 239.

19 Walt Brown Jr., ed., *An American for Lafayette: The Diaries of E. C. C. Genet* (Charlottesville: University Press of Virginia, 1981), 19.

19 Ibid., 129.

19 Ibid., 180.

20 MacDonald, 139.

20–21 Marie A. V. Speakman, *Memories* (Wilmington, DE: Greenwood Bookshop, 1937), 24,

21 Ibid., 175.

21 Minne Allen and Edward Allen, *Tenderness & Turmoil: Letters to a German Mother, 1914–1920* (Santa Ana, CA: Seven Locks Press, 1998), 149.

24 Bankers Trust Company, *America's Attitude Toward the War* (New York: Bankers Trust Company, 1917), 37.

25 Ibid., 99.

25 Ibid., 114.

25 Ibid., 119.

25 Ibid.

26 Ibid., 119, 121.

27 James H. Hallas, *Doughboy War: The American Expeditionary Force in World War I* (Boulder, CO: Lynne Rienner, 2000), 9.

27 Alexander W. Moffat, *Maverick Navy* (Middletown, CT: Wesleyan University Press, 1976), 12.

28 Ibid., 16.

29 W. Alison Sweeney, *History of the American Negro in the Great World War* (1919; repr., New York: Johnson, 1970), 108, 106.

29–30 Ibid., 137.

32 Hallas, 9.

32 Ibid.

32 George B. Clark, ed., *His Time in Hell: A Texas Marine in France*

(Novato, CA: Presidio Press, 2001), 4.

32 Charles MacArthur, *War Bugs* (Garden City, NY: Doubleday, Doran & Company, 1929), 3.

33 Stillman F. Westbrook, *Those Eighteen Months* (Hartford, CT: Cases, Lockwood & Brainard, 1929), 4.

33 Louis Felix Ranlett, *Let's Go: The Story of A. S. No. 2448602* (Boston: Houghton Mifflin, 1927), 12.

33 Ray DeWitt Herring, *Trifling with War* (Boston: Meador Publishing, 1934), 15, 18.

34 Ibid.

34 Frank Freidel, *Over There: The Story of America's First Great Overseas Crusade*, rev. ed. (Philadelphia: Temple University Press, 1990), 31–32.

34 Ibid.

35 William L. Langer, *Gas and Flame in World War I* (New York: Alfred A. Knopf, 1965), xix.

36 John J. Pershing, *My Experiences in the World War* vol. 2, (New York: Frederick A. Stokes, 1931), 32–33.

36 Brian W. Harvey and Carol Fitzgerald, eds., *Edward Heron-Allen's Journal of the Great War* (Chichester, UK: Phillimore & Co., 2002), 86.

37 Langer, xxi.

37 Herring, 42.

37 Malcolm Brown, *The Imperial War Museum Book of the Western Front* (London: Sidgwick & Jackson, 1993), 237.

37 Herring, 90.

39 Freidel, 50.

40 Byron Farwell, *Over There: The United States in the Great War 1917–1918* (New York: W. W. Norton, 1999), 19–20.

40 Ibid.

40 Ibid., 37.

40–41 Hunter Liggett, *The A.E.F.—Ten Years Ago in France* (New York: Dodd, Mead & Company, 1928), 50.

41–42 Pershing, 32–33.

42 James Luby, ed., *One Who Gave His Life: War Letters of Quincy Sharpe Mills* (New York: G. P. Putnam's Sons, 1923), 356.

43 *Stars and Stripes* "There's a Reason," no. 01 (Feb. 8, 1918): 3.

43 William Hazlett Upson, *Me and Henry and the Artillery* (New York: Doubleday, Doran & Company, 1928), 12.

44 Luby, 355.

44 Joseph Douglas Lawrence, *Fighting Soldier: The AEF in 1918* (Boulder: Colorado Associated University Press, 1985), 79.

44 MacArthur, 15.

45 Clark, 38.

45 Herring, 23.

46 Clark, 97.

46 *Stars and Stripes,* "There's A Reason," 3.

47 Speakman, 168.

48 Daniel A. Poling, *Huts in Hell* (Boston: Christian Endeavor World, 1918), 38.

48 *Stars and Stripes* "G.H.Q. Fights Rum in General Order," no. 44 (Dec. 6, 1918): 5.

49 Ernst Jünger, *The Storm of Steel* (New York: Howard Fertig, 1996), 51.

49 Ibid., 52.

51 Carl Andrew Brannen, *Over There: A Marine in the Great War* (College Station: Texas A & M University Press, 1996), 21.

51 Clark, 55.

51 Abbey, 90.

52 Brannen, 55.

53 *Stars and Stripes* "Trenchfoot," no. 3 (Feb. 22, 1918): 5.

53 Ibid.

54 MacDonald, 292.

54 Stuart McGuire, *History of U.S. Army Base Hospital No. 45 in the Great War* (Richmond: William Byrd, 1924), 252.

54 Ranlett, 81–82.

56 Farwell, 43.

57 Brannen, 21.

57 Poling, 98.

57 Ibid.

57 Ibid., 96.

58 Langer, 34.

59 Elton E. Mackin, *Suddenly We Didn't Want to Die* (Novato, CA: Presidio Press, 1993), 183.

60 MacArthur, 175–176.

60 Will Judy, *A Soldier's Diary* (Chicago: Judy Publishing, 1930), 151.

61 Ibid.

61 Freidel, rev. ed. 75.

62 *Stars and Stripes* "Yes, the Kaiser's Sure We're on the Western Front Now," no. 5 (March 18, 1918): 1.

62 Freidel, 1st ed. 136–137.

63 Ian F. D. Morrow, trans., *Rudolf Binding, a Fatalist at War* (Boston: Houghton Mifflin, 1929), 221.

63 Ibid.

64 Brannen, 21.

64 Freidel 1st ed., 193–194.

64 Ibid.

64 J. Stuart Richards, ed., *Pennsylvanian Voices of the Great War* (Jefferson, NC: McFarland, 2002), 59.

65 Farwell, 173.

65 Richards, 60.

65 Ibid.

66 Luby, 448.

66 Svetlana Palmer and Sarah Wallis, eds., *Intimate Voices from the First World War* (New York: William Morrow, 2003), 324–325.

66 MacArthur, 166–167.

68 Jean Bernard Villars, *Notes of a Lost Pilot* (Hamden, CT: Archon Books, 1975), 127.

69 David K. Vaughan, *Flying for the Air Service: The Hughes Brothers in World War I* (Bowling Green, OH: Bowling Green State University Popular Press, 1998), 144.

69 Villars, 127.

70 William M. Wright, *Meuse-Argonne Diary* (Columbia: University of Missouri Press, 2004), 40.

71 MacArthur, 175–176.

72 Langer, 77.

72 Ranlett, 290.

72 Terry M. Bareither, *An Engineer's Diary of the Great War* (West Lafayette, IN: Purdue University Press, 2002), 102.

73 MacArthur, 183.

74 Robert Hoffman, *I Remember the Last War* (York, PA: Strength & Health, 1940), 165–166.

74 Mackin, 44.

74 Morrow, 65.

74 Bareither, 105.

74 Jünger, 23.

75 Hoffman, 165–166.

76 Guy Emerson Bowerman Jr., *The Compensations of War* (Austin: University of Texas Press, 1983), 32.

76 MacDonald, 284.

77 Bishop and Bostridge, 368.

77 Richards, 61.

78 *Stars and Stripes* "Huns Starve and Ridicule U.S. Captives," no. 1 (Feb. 8, 1918): 1.

79 Ibid.

79 Robert Jackson, *The Prisoners, 1914–18* (London: Routledge, 1989), 151–152.

80 Margaret R. Higgonet, *Nurses at the Front: Writing the Wounds of the Great War* (Boston: Northeastern University Press, 2001), 151.

81 Louise Elliott Dalby, *The Great War and Women's Liberation* (Saratoga, NY: Skidmore College Faculty Research Lecture, 1970), 25.

82 Lettie Gavin, *American Women in World War I: They Also Served* (Niwot: University Press of Colorado, 1997), 2.

82 Ibid., 26.

84 Higgonet, 7.

84 Susan R. Grayzel, *Women and the First World War* (London: Longman, 2002), 41.

85 Higgonet, 151.

85 Margaret Lambie, *Verdun Experiences* (Washington, DC: Courant Press, 1945), 30.

85 Gavin, 103

86 Ibid.

87 Ibid.

87 Grayzel, 108.

87 Dalby, 27.

88 Upson, 271.

88 Frederick Palmer, *My Year of the Great War* (New York: Dodd, Mead & Company, 1917), 90.

88 Palmer and Wallis, 358.

88–89 Morrow, 244.

89 Allen and Allen, 186.

89–90 Wright, 165.

90 Ibid.

90 Westbrook, 39.

90 *Stars and Stripes* "Guns along the Meuse Roar Grand Finale of Eleventh Houur [sic]," no. 41 (November 15, 1918): 1.

90 Ibid.

91 Lonnie J. White, *Panthers to Arrowheads: The 36th Division in World War I* (Austin, TX: Presidial Press, 1984), 212.

92 Mike Roden, "Welcome Home," *Aftermath: When the Boys Came Home,* 2002, www.aftermathww1.com (July 30, 2005).

93 Jennifer D. Keene, *Doughboys, the Great War and the Remaking of America* (Baltimore: Johns Hopkins University Press, 2001), 205.

95 Addie W. Hunton and Kathryn M. Johnson, *Two Colored Women with the American Expeditionary Forces* (New York: AMS Press, 1971), 26, 29.

95 Liggett, 50.

96 René Arnaud, *My Funny Little War* (Cranbury, NJ: A. S. Barnes, 1967), 154.

96 Ibid.

97 Upson, 271.

BIBLIOGRAPHY

Abbey, Edwin Austin. *An American Soldier*. Boston: Houghton Mifflin Company, 1918.

Allen, Minne, and Edward Allen. *Tenderness & Turmoil: Letters to a German Mother, 1914–1920*. Santa Ana, CA: Seven Locks Press, 1998.

Arnaud, René. *My Funny Little War*. Cranbury, NJ: A. S. Barnes, 1967.

Bankers Trust Company. *America's Attitude Toward the War*. New York: Bankers Trust Company, 1917.

Bareither, Terry M. *An Engineer's Diary of the Great War*. West Lafayette, IN: Purdue University Press, 2002.

Bishop, Alan, and Mark Bostridge, eds. *Letters from a Lost Generation*. Boston: Northeastern University Press, 1998.

Bowerman, Guy Emerson, Jr. *The Compensations of War*. Austin: University of Texas Press, 1983.

Brannen, Carl Andrew. *Over There: A Marine in the Great War*. College Station: Texas A & M University Press, 1996.

Brown, Malcolm. *The Imperial War Museum Book of The First World War*. Norman: University of Oklahoma Press, 1993.

——. *The Imperial War Museum Book of the Western Front*. London: Sidgwick & Jackson, 1993.

Brown, Walt, Jr., ed. *An American for Lafayette: The Diaries of E. C. C. Genet*. Charlottesville: University Press of Virginia, 1981.

Clark, George B., ed. *His Time in Hell: A Texas Marine in France*. Novato, CA: Presidio Press, 2001.

Connes, George. *A POW's Memoir of the First World War*. Oxford, UK: Berg, 2004.

Dalby, Louise Elliott. *The Great War and Women's Liberation*. Saratoga, NY: Skidmore College Faculty Research Lecture, 1970.

Farwell, Byron. *Over There: The United States in the Great War 1917–1918*. New York: W. W. Norton, 1999.

Freidel, Frank. *Over There: The Story of America's First Great Overseas Crusade*. New York: Bramhall House, 1964.

Freidel, Frank. *Over There: The Story of America's First Great Overseas Crusade*. Revised edition. Philadelphia: Temple University Press, 1990.

Gavin, Lettie. *American Women in World War I: They Also Served*. Niwot: University Press of Colorado, 1997.

Giffard, Sydney. *Guns, Kites and Horses*. London: Radcliffe Press, 2003.

Grayzel, Susan R. *Women and the First World War*. London: Longman, 2002.

Hallas, James H. *Doughboy War: The American Expeditionary Force in World War I*. Boulder, CO: Lynne Rienner, 2000.

Harvey, Brian W., and Carol Fitzgerald, eds. *Edward Heron-Allen's Journal of the Great War*. Chichester, UK: Phillimore & Co. Ltd, 2002.

Herring, Ray DeWitt. *Trifling with War*. Boston: Meador Publishing, 1934.

Higgonet, Margaret R. *Nurses at the Front: Writing the Wounds of the Great War*. Boston: Northeastern University Press, 2001.

Hoffman, Robert. *I Remember the Last War*. York, PA: Strength & Health, 1940.

Hunton, Addie W., and Kathryn M. Johnson. *Two Colored Women with the American Expeditionary Forces*. New York: AMS Press, 1971.

Jackson, Robert. *The Prisoners, 1914–18*. London: Routledge, 1989.

Judy, Will. *A Soldier's Diary*. Chicago: Judy Publishing, 1930.

Jünger, Ernst. *The Storm of Steel*. New York: Howard Fertig, 1996.

Keene, Jennifer D. *Doughboys, the Great War and the Remaking of America*. Baltimore: John Hopkins University Press, 2001.

Lambie, Margaret. *Verdun Experiences*. Washington, DC: Courant Press, 1945.

Langer, William L. *Gas and Flame in World War I*. New York: Alfred A. Knopf, 1965.

Lawrence, Joseph Douglas. *Fighting Soldier: The AEF in 1918*. Boulder: Colorado Associated University Press, 1985.

Libby, Frederick. *Horses Don't Fly*. New York: Arcade Publishing, 2000.

Liggett, Hunter. *The A.E.F.—Ten Years Ago in France*. New York: Dodd, Mead and Company, 1928.

Luby, James, ed. *One Who Gave His Life: War Letters of Quincy Sharpe Mills*. New York: G. P. Putnam's Sons, 1923.

MacArthur, Charles. *War Bugs*. Garden City, NY: Doubleday, Doran & Company, 1929.

MacDonald, Lyn. *The Roses of No Man's Land*. London: Michael Joseph, 1980.

Mackin, Elton E. *Suddenly We Didn't Want to Die*. Novato, CA: Presidio Press, 1993.

Mallett, Christian. *Impressions and Experiences of a French Trooper 1914–1915*. London: Constable & Company, 1916.

McGuire, Stuart. *History of U.S. Army Base Hospital No. 45 in the Great War*. Richmond: William Byrd, 1924.

Mead, Gary. *The Doughboys: America and the First World War*. Woodstock, NY: Overlook Press, 2000.

Moffat, Alexander W. *Maverick Navy*. Middletown, CT: Wesleyan University Press, 1976.

Morrow, Ian F. D., trans. *Rudolf Binding, a Fatalist at War*. Boston: Houghton Mifflin Company, 1929.

Palmer, Frederick. *My Year of the Great War*. New York: Dodd, Mead and Company, 1917.

Palmer, Svetlana, and Sarah Wallis, eds. *Intimate Voices from the First World War*. New York: William Morrow, 2003.

Pershing, John J. *My Experiences in the World War*. vol. 2. New York, Frederick A. Stokes, 1931.

Poling, Daniel A. *Huts in Hell*. Boston: Christian Endeavor World, 1918.

Ranlett, Louis Felix. *Let's Go: The Story of A. S. No. 2448602*. Boston: Houghton Mifflin, 1927.

Read, I. L. *Of Those We Loved*. Edinburgh, UK: Pentland Press, 1994.

Redier, Antoine. *Comrades in Courage*. Garden City, NY: Doubleday, Page & Company, 1918.

Richards, J. Stuart, ed. *Pennsylvanian Voices of the Great War*. Jefferson, NC: McFarland, 2002.

Richter, Donald C., ed. *Lionel Sotheby's Great War*. Athens: Ohio University Press, 1997.

Speakman, Marie A. V. *Memories*. Wilmington, DE: Greenwood Bookshop, 1937.

Sweeney, W. Alison. *History of the American Negro in the Great World War*. 1919. Reprint, New York: Johnson, 1970.

Upson, William Hazlett. *Me and Henry and the Artillery*. New York: Doubleday, Doran and Company, 1928.

Vaughan, David K. *Flying for the Air Service: The Hughes Brothers in World War I*. Bowling Green, OH: Bowling Green State University Popular Press, 1998.

Villars, Jean Bernard. *Notes of a Lost Pilot*. Hamden, CT: Archon Books, 1975.

Westbrook, Stillman F. *Those Eighteen Months*. Hartford, CT: Cases, Lockwood & Brainard, 1929.

White, Lonnie J. *Panthers to Arrowheads: The 36th Division in World War I*. Austin, TX: Presidial Press, 1984.

Wright, William M. *Meuse-Argonne Diary*. Columbia: University of Missouri Press, 2004.

Zieger, Robert H. *America's Great War*. Lanham, MD: Rowman & Littlefield, 2000.

For Further Information

Books

Adams, Simon. *World War I*. New York: DK Children, 2007.

Bosco, Peter I. *World War I*. New York: Facts On File, 2003.

Dommermuth-Costa, Carol. *Woodrow Wilson*. Minneapolis: Twenty-First Century Books, 2003.

Feldman, Ruth Tenzer. *World War I*. Minneapolis: Twenty-First Century Books, 2004.

Gilbert, Adrian. *Going to War in World War I*. Danbury, CT: Franklin Watts, 2001.

Gourley, Catherine. *Gibson Girls and Suffragists*. Minneapolis: Twenty-First Century Books, 2008.

Kent, Zachary. *World War I: The War to End Wars*. Berkeley Heights, NJ: Enslow Publishers, 2000.

Ruggiero, Adriane. *American Voices from World War I*. Tarrytown, NY: Benchmark Books, 2003.

Schomp, Virginia. *World War I*. Tarrytown, NY: Benchmark Books, 2004.

Taylor, David. *Key Battles of World War I*. Oxford, UK: Heinemann Library, 2001.

Whiting, Jim. *An Overview of World War I*. Hockessin, DE: Mitchell Lane Publishers, 2006.

Zeinart, Karen. *Those Extraordinary Women of World War I*. Minneapolis: Twenty-First Century Books, 2001.

Internet Resources

Aftermath: When the Boys Came Home
    http://www.aftermathwwl.com
    This website memorializes those who fought in the war and discusses how the world changed after the war.

Dear Home: Letters From World War I
    http://www.historychannel.com/letters/wwiletters.html
    This website displays actual letters from the people who served in World War I, including troops and nurses.

Douaumont Ossuary
    http://www.verdun-douaumont.com/en/index.html
    This is the official website of the Douaumont Ossuary, which contains the remains of 130,000 soldiers who died on the battlefields of World War I.

The Great War and the Shaping of the 20th Century
    http://www.pbs.org/greatwar/
    This World War I website gives more details about the war, including time-lines, maps, audio, and historians' commentaries.

The Great War: 80 Years On
> http://news.bbc.co.uk/1/hi/special_report/1998/10/98/world_war_i/197437.stm
>
> This BBC news website contains many articles, letters, and radio interviews about World War I.

Stars and Stripes: The American Soldiers' Newspaper of World War I, 1918–1919
> http://memory.loc.gov/ammem/sgphtml/sashtml/sashome.html
>
> This is a collection of articles from *Stars and Stripes*, the newspaper for U.S. troops during World War I.

The War to End All Wars
> http://www.firstworldwar.com
>
> This World War I website contains articles, battlefield tours, maps, memoirs and diaries, photographs, timelines, and a who's who gallery.

World War I: Trenches on the Web
> http://www.worldwar1.com
>
> This site provides information on the people, places, and events of World War I.

INDEX

ABOUT THE AUTHOR

Susan Provost Beller is the author of twenty history books for young readers. She writes from her home in Charlotte, Vermont, when she is not either traveling to see historic sites or visiting with her three children and five grandchildren. Her one wish is that someone would invent a time machine so she could go back and really see the past!

PHOTO ACKNOWLEDGMENTS

The images in this book are used with the permission of: © Laura Westlund/Independent Picture Service, pp. 1, 2–3, 98, all sidebar backgrounds; National Archives, pp. 2 (NWDNS-111-SC-14863), 29 (NWDNS-111-SC-9362), 30 (NWDNS-165-WW-127-8), 52 (W&C 666), 58 (NWDNS-111-SC-18706), 67 (NWDNS-111-SC-24516), 70 (W&C 497), 71 (W&C 620), 86 (W&C 545), 89 (W&C 711), 92 (W&C 720), 95 (W&C 717); © Hulton Archive/Getty Images, pp. 7, 12, 20, 32, 55, 69, 77, 84; © LL/Roger Viollet/Getty Images, p. 11; © Underwood & Underwood/CORBIS, p. 15; Library of Congress, pp. 18 (LC-USZ62-111663), 22 (LC-USZ62-76929), 24 (LC-USZ62-21728), 45 (LC-USZ62-98320), 62 (LC-USZ62-51352), 81 (LC-USZ62-115697); © Hulton-Deutsch Collection/CORBIS, p. 23; © Topical Press Agency/Hulton Archive/Getty Images, p. 34; © A.R. Costar/Topical Press Agency/Hulton Archive/Getty Images, p. 39; Library of Congress, Serial and Government Publications Division, p. 46; © MPI/Hulton Archive/Getty Images, pp. 56, 65; © Bettmann/CORBIS, p. 75; Courtesy of the National Library of Medicine, p. 85; © CORBIS, p. 91; American Battle Monuments Commission, Arlington, VA, p. 94.

Front Cover: © Bill Wilson/The Anniston Star, used with the permission of the City of Anniston, Alabama (statue); © Laura Westlund/Independent Picture Service (background).